THE
Messiah's
Servant

READER VIEWS
★ ★ ★
Bronze
★ ★ ★
REVIEWERS CHOICE AWARDS

WILLIAM I. BRAZLEY, JR.

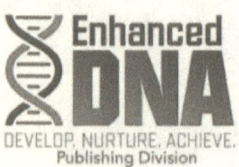

Enhanced DNA
DEVELOP. NURTURE. ACHIEVE.
Publishing Division

The Messiah's Servant

Copyright © 2021 William I. Brazley, Jr.

All rights reserved.

Credit: Editing by Michelle P. Jones, Inc.

Cover by Marvin Rhodes (MR Designs)

ISBN-13: 978-1-7360431-6-5
Library of Congress Number: 2021903936

ACKNOWLEDGEMENTS

First, I want to thank my Lord and Savior, Jesus Christ, for giving me the inspiration to write this book, and the focus to complete it. I can do all things through Christ who strengthens me. *Philippians 4:13*

I am dedicating this book to my mother, Gwendolyn, and my wife Frances. Long before my mother relocated to Glory in 2010, she raised seven bad kids as a single parent. She put the fear of God in all of us at an early age…one way or another. My wife Frances is the most sincere, dedicated believer that I know. She supports my creative endeavors and inspires me to be the best version of myself I can possibly be.

I want to thank all of my friends and family, including my church family. You are too many to list but you are never forgotten. All of you have said something at one point in time to encourage me, whether you realize it or not. I thank God for you.

I am not a pastor, deacon, or even an eloquent speaker, but I am a believer. As believers, we are instructed to share Christ with as many people as we can. *The Messiah's Servant* is my attempt to do just that. The story is fictional but the message and the scriptures are real. I hope that you enjoy the story, but I pray that you believe and remember the message.

CHAPTER 1

CALLED TO SERVE

Jesus' journey was almost at its end, and it had been physically and mentally tough— physically tough because he was sore and bloody from the beating he had taken, and mentally tough because he had to fight off the urge to use his power to prevent the verbal and physical abuse he received. His open wounds and swollen eyes made it difficult to navigate the dirt road that stretched out before him. He struggled to walk a path he knew well but had never traveled. The strength of his body quickly faded. The cross he carried on his shoulder, and the fact that his back was lacerated and bleeding, had a lot to do with his physical decline.

Two others who carried crosses over their shoulders would suffer the same fate, but they were not beaten beforehand. They did not have the open wounds that were streaming blood. They did not wear a crown of thorns that had been pressed into their scalp. They were not the ones the crowd had gathered to see. No one had ever called either of them Lord.

Each step became more and more difficult, and his strength began to give out. He collapsed to one knee and used all the strength he had to keep from falling over.

"My Jesus!" cried out a woman from the crowd.

A man rushed to the carpenter's side and steadied him. He felt the blood from the carpenter's wounds ooze over his fingers, hands, and wrists as he held him. Jesus made eye contact with the kind stranger, and the man could not look away. Although Jesus did not open his mouth, the stranger could hear him very plainly:

"You will be remembered for your kindness, Simon of Cyrene."

Simon was bewildered. Was he imagining this? Did he just hear Jesus speak to him? He did not see this man move his mouth. He knew who Jesus claimed to be, but how did Jesus know him? He thought about this for a moment and decided there was only one reasonable explanation: the stories he had heard had some truth to them. Was Jesus really the Messiah, the son of the living God? Simon felt a rush of different emotions that he could not explain.

A Roman centurion approached on horseback. He looked down on them with a scowl of arrogance that reeked of authority. A foot soldier hurriedly approached them with his whip raised and ready to strike. The centurion raised his hand in disapproval, and the soldier backed away.

"What is your name, my friend?"

"I am Simon of Cyrene," said the stranger.

"Why is Simon of Cyrene interfering with the business of Rome?"

"Interference is not my intention, sir. I am merely trying to show this man a little compassion before Rome concludes its business with Him."

"Maybe you should show your compassion by carrying his cross."

Simon could tell that the centurion's words were more of a command than a suggestion. This was confirmed when two foot-soldiers came in close with their hands on the hilt of their swords. Simon carried a bag of dried meat and a large knife around his waist. He was certain that the bag of meat was not what the soldiers were focusing on. The large knife was obvious and was probably the reason the foot soldiers had taken an offensive stance. Instinct warned him to move slowly and cautiously.

Simon did as he was instructed. He helped remove the cross from the shoulder of Jesus and helped Him to his feet. His hands became completely covered with the blood that was streaming down the Messiah's back. Once Jesus was steady on his feet, Simon positioned the cross on his shoulder and slowly followed Jesus up the hill. Their journey came to an end at a place called the Skull, also known as Calvary.

"I suggest you leave now unless you want to share the cross with your friend," ordered the centurion.

Simon pushed the cross to the ground and backed away. He blended in with the crowd and decided to stay and witness the execution. The onlookers were allowed to come only so close. A good number of them were as close as they dared to come, fearing death by association. The crowd was emotionally charged. Some had a thirst for blood and wanted to see an execution. Others wailed and cried in absolute horror. Some did not know what to think or what to believe. Then some were frightened that this man might actually be who He said He was. They were the ones who plotted against him, the ones who had self-serving motives, the ones who would burn forever.

The majestic but bruised and bloody Messiah turned and looked at Simon while the foot soldiers removed his clothes and prepared his cross. Once again, Simon and Jesus made eye contact, and once again, Simon was captured in the gaze of Christ. Again, the voice of Jesus became clear and distinct communication in the mind of Simon:

"You are a kind and caring man, Simon of Cyrene. I have work for you to do. Are you ready to go to work?"

Simon was confused, wondering if this was real. He could not break the eye contact. The eyes of Jesus were hypnotic and piercing. The few seconds that passed seemed much longer than they actually were. He did not understand what was happening, but he was not frightened. "Yes!" he replied, not realizing that he had spoken out boldly and that the people around him had heard him. His timing was not ideal because it was at that precise moment that the foot soldiers grabbed Jesus and laid him down on the cross. Some loyal followers who heard Simon's reply became upset. They believed that he was approving of the crucifixion. His blood-covered hands justified their beliefs.

Simon began to back away from the crowd. He tried to wipe the blood on his shirt, but it would not leave his hands. The blood still looked wet, but it did not wipe off. He noticed how bright and vibrant the blood was. It was so bright it almost glowed. At that moment a scream pierced the air. To his dismay, the soldiers had just nailed Jesus' left hand to the cross. He saw a foot soldier hit the metal stake twice more before heading over to the Messiah's right hand. Simon could not bear to watch. He looked for an exit route. People moved out of his way as he hurriedly made his way through the crowd. They did not know what to think of this tall, muscular, dark-skinned man approaching them with bloody hands. As soon as he was able to break into a full run, he heard another scream of pain, followed by continuous moans of agony. Simon ran as fast as he could for as long as he could.

He ran for twenty or thirty minutes without stopping and without looking back. His physical limits overpowered his mental anguish, and he began to slow down. Simon came to a stop near a large tree. It took him another twenty minutes to catch his breath. He forgot about the rest of the Passover festivities, which was the reason for his visit. He could not forget the sight and sound of the suffering Jesus. Resting his back against the tree, Simon looked at his hands and wondered what work he had agreed to do. Jesus did not get a chance to tell him. He slid down the trunk of the tree and sat on the ground. He was physically and mentally exhausted. He wanted to go home. It was still early in the day, but he felt as if he had labored all day.

He stared at his hands for what seemed to be mere minutes. Without warning, his hands began to change right before his eyes. The bright red blood began to look dull and dirty. Within moments, the blood looked as if it had been dried for days. The sudden fading of sunlight caused Simon to look away from his hands and examine the sky. The bright daylight had turned into a darkness that he had never experienced before. The wind picked up, and he knew a storm was blowing in. He was sure of it when the lightning flashed, but it flashed only over the area from which he had just run. He was convinced that this had something to do with the crucifixion of Jesus. He had heard about some of the miracles Jesus had performed; miracles made possible through God, the Father. Simon was becoming nervous. Maybe the Father was avenging the son. He looked around for a place to take cover, a place to hide. There was no such place. He brought his knees up to his chest, wrapped his arms around his legs, and placed his forehead on his knees. Then he waited for the storm to run its course. He would never forget this moment, this darkness in the middle of the day, this black Friday.

A few hours passed with no change. At times he thought the wind would carry him away. It hurled the raindrops like darts, with a force that made him cover his face. He could not raise his head. It was as if he were being forced to keep his head bowed in reverence. Occasional claps of thunder caused him to jump every time he heard them. He had never heard thunder so loud and so close. Though his eyes were closed, he could still see the flashes of lightning. It did not feel as close as the thunder, and he knew it was concentrated over the area of the crucifixion.

Time crept by as the storm finally lost a lot of its energy. The wind calmed down, and the rain was barely noticeable. The occasional clap of thunder and bolt of lightning always caught Simon by surprise. He decided to sit still for a while longer. He was scared and confused and used the time to gather his thoughts, trying to make sense out of everything that had happened.

As the clouds scattered and the darkness dissipated, he raised his head. There was still enough daylight remaining for him to put a lot of distance between this place and himself. He did not realize how tight

5

he had been squeezing his legs until he tried to stand. He stretched and massaged his legs to regain the feeling in them. He stood and looked around for a couple of minutes to get his bearing, and then he began his trek home. He was a little stiff, but he could slowly feel the circulation returning to his legs. As his legs got stronger, his pace quickened.

He walked about as far as he could and then began to look for a place to lay his head. His pace had slowed considerably, not because of physical exertion but from a lack of light. The darkness was similar to that which followed the crucifixion of Jesus. This darkness was complete; there wasn't a star in the sky. Simon was finding it difficult to see where his feet landed. He slowly felt his way along until he came to a large tree. Normally he would have spent the night up in the tree, but it was impossible for him to see his way to climb it. He figured it would be safe for him to lie down near its base. It was unlikely that anyone or anything could manipulate this darkness. He closed his eyes and quickly fell asleep.

Saturday morning came sooner than Simon expected. He was more tired than he thought. It was far from dawn, but the first hint of light had awakened him. His eyes were still adjusting as he surveyed the territory around him. He was familiar with his surroundings and knew exactly where he was. As he continued his trek home, his stomach reminded him that he had not eaten anything in a while. He grabbed a few pieces of dried meat from his bag and ate as he walked.

He walked all day Saturday and made good time. He had another week of travel left before he would reach Cyrene, but he knew that he had only about thirty minutes of sunlight remaining in the day. Simon decided that the tree in front of him was as good as any. His travel the next day would be long and hot, so he concentrated on where he could find water. He climbed halfway up the tree and got comfortable on a large sturdy branch. He relaxed and finished the remainder of his meat.

After the storm ceased Friday night, his journey had been uneventful. That was a blessing because he had been lost in thought the entire day. Any type of aggression from a man or animal would have caught him completely by surprise. He was operating basically on instinct. He was focused on the thoughts Jesus had planted in his head. Would he ever find the answers he sought, or would those thoughts haunt him for the rest of his life? Those were Simon's last thoughts as he dozed off to sleep.

Sunday rolled in quickly, thought Simon, as he rubbed his face. It seemed as if he had just closed his eyes. He must have overslept; there was too much sunlight beaming down. Simon expected to be looking into a bright sun when he opened his eyes, but he was surprised to discover there wasn't any daylight. The bright light was coming from his hands. The dried blood had become bright red once again. It looked as if the blood was fresh, but it was still dry. He stared at his hands in amazement. He struggled to understand what was happening. Was Jesus haunting him? The blood of Jesus that oozed over his hands three days ago had become vibrant and alive again. What was the meaning of this?

It was at least an hour before sun-up, and Simon spent the entire time looking at his hands, trying to figure out why the blood looked fresh again. Not only did the brightness of the blood swallow the darkness around it, but his hands pulsated with energy and power. How could such power be found in such a humble man's blood? Once more he reflected on the stories he had heard about Jesus—his miraculous healing power, unmatched wisdom, and claims of deity. Once again, he rationalized that maybe Jesus was indeed the son of the living God. That explained the power he felt coursing through his body. He almost fell from the tree when the voice of Jesus spoke to his mind:

"The harvest is plentiful, but the workers are few. It is time to go to work, Simon of Cyrene. Say goodbye to your family, then head south."

Could this be real? Was he going mad? First, his hands turned bright red again, and then Jesus spoke to him from the grave. He felt his cheeks and forehead to see if he was burning with fever. Maybe he was sick or hallucinating. What should he do? He was anxious to see his sons, but he had just been instructed to leave his family. He forced himself to focus, to try to remember everything he had heard about Jesus. He could not think clearly. He was excited, confused, and concerned all at the same time.

Slowly he started to regain his focus. He tried to put a logical spin on everything he had been through the last few days, but logic wasn't holding up. He sat in deep thought for a few minutes, not knowing what to do. He did not know what his future held, but for some reason he trusted Jesus. Somehow, he knew he would be alright. He couldn't explain it; he just felt it. He could not ignore the calling of the Messiah.

Time passed quickly. The sun was up, and Simon knew that he should have been on the road at least thirty minutes ago. He climbed down from the tree and walked as swiftly as he could. Jesus said he could say goodbye to his family, and he planned to do just that. He hoped his parting would be temporary, but deep down inside he knew differently.

He walked for three hours before slowing down. He tried to cover as much ground as he could before stopping. His pace was fast, and he took every shortcut that he knew, including a path through the bush. Cyrene was a mountainous city, and the scenery from its hillsides was breathtaking. However, to get to it, you had to either travel through the bush or take the longer route through the mountains. The bush was gorgeous and full of exotic animals, many of which could easily kill a man.

Stories about Jesus raced through his head. Stories of miracles, of healing, of love, and persuasion all filled his head. He did not know much about Jesus, only what he had heard from others. He was struggling to remember something about the blood of Jesus. If only he could remember. Wait a minute; something was coming to mind. He had once heard someone say that His blood was shed for our sins.

What was that about? Why did that phrase pop into his head? On second thought, he had never heard that before. Jesus just died days ago. He had heard that Jesus was killed because he wanted to be king, but Rome already had a king, a tyrant of a king. Jesus was labeled as King of the Jews; or did he claim to be King of the Jews?

Simon was getting confused. Phrases, gossip, and incidents filled his head. Most of these he had never heard or experienced before. The faster he walked, the more he remembered. But how could he remember something he never knew in the first place? Something was happening to him. First, he heard the voice of Jesus in his head, but the lips of Jesus did not move. Then he heard the voice of Jesus again after he had been killed. Now he was remembering things he never knew in the first place. There was only one explanation: Jesus had cursed him. He was going mad.

Something moved in Simon's peripheral vision, and he immediately stopped. He slowly turned his head toward his left shoulder and saw a male lion about twenty feet away. As he slowly placed his hand on his knife, he noticed another lion not far from the first one; both were standing perfectly still and watching him. He had a chance of surviving one lion, a slight chance but still a chance. There was no way he could survive the attack of two. He slowly backed away from the lions, trying to find a tree in which he could take refuge. His heart beat harder as he fought off the panic rising in him. Not only was the closest tree too far away for him to reach, but as he looked around, he saw that he was surrounded by lions. There had to be at least ten to twelve lions within striking distance. He had never seen so many gathered for one kill. He wasn't scared of death, but to go out like this would be pretty painful. He knew he would never see his sons again and prayed they would not forget their father.

"Not only will your sons remember you, but you will forever be remembered as the only person not afraid to show Me kindness and compassion in My darkest hour. Continue your journey. Your work still awaits you."

The voice of Jesus was so clear and distinct that Simon turned suddenly, expecting to see someone on the other side of him. To his dismay, no one was there. Now, he was sure he had gone mad. That explained everything. He would die a madman, devoured by lions. There would not be enough of him left for anyone to figure out what happened to him. He had to be mad. Why did Jesus tell him to continue his journey when he was about to die? He could not explain the blood or the voice of a dead man, but none of that mattered now.

He decided he would go out fighting. He knew he would not survive, but maybe he could wound at least one of them before he was overcome. He knew it would have to be whichever one struck first because the mere weight of any one of them would incapacitate him. He slowly withdrew his knife from its sheath and held it out in front of him, as he tried to determine which one would strike first. He waited to begin his final battle.

Something was wrong. Nothing was happening. Not a single lion had approached him. They all kept their distance and continued to look at him. He slowly made a 360-degree turn, and each lion seemed more curious than hungry. Then he noticed something. As he slowly moved, the head of each lion turned and followed his every movement. More specifically, they seemed to have noticed his blood-stained hands. They were following the movement of his hands.

Simon tested this theory very slowly, trying not to appear aggressive. He raised both of his hands above his head, and like well-synchronized choreography, each lion looked up at them. He slowly lowered his hands to his side, and each lion followed their movement. He was perplexed. He did not know what to think. After standing perfectly still for a few moments, the lions started to make eye contact, as if to be asking what was next. Simon himself wondered the same thing.

His thoughts went back to Christ. The strange behavior of the lions had something to do with Jesus. He was sure of it. Maybe Jesus was trying to tell him that he would be okay, that they would not harm him. Continuing to be extremely cautious, he slowly continued his journey. Keeping their distance, the lions began to walk in a line on each side of him. A few of them walked directly behind him, forming a big U formation with Simon in the middle of it. It was as if they were escorting him, even protecting him. It must be Jesus, he thought. He was aware of some of the miracles people claimed Jesus had performed, and now he had witnessed one firsthand.

Suddenly, Simon was overcome with emotion, and all concern left him. He felt relaxed and extremely confident. The Spirit of Jesus had entered him. He did not understand what was happening to him, but he would soon be knowledgeable of the Holy Spirit. He was experiencing a peace he had never felt before. Without a doubt, he had become a believer. Placing his knife back in its sheath, he dropped to his knees and began to pray. Surprisingly, each lion knelt down when he did. Simon confessed, "Jesus Christ is Lord. I will trust in the Lord until I die."

When he stood up, so did each lion. He looked at them for the first time without fear and began to notice their beauty. These big, powerful animals were magnificent and wonderfully made. He looked them over until he spotted the largest one in the group, the alpha male. He made eye contact with the huge killing machine. "Come here," he commanded. The massive lion slowly walked over to Simon and stopped right in front of him. He took a couple of steps toward the lion and rubbed him on the head, then stroked his huge mane. The lion seemed to approve. He stepped toward Simon and rubbed his head against his body.

As he continued his journey, his new feline friend stayed right beside him. He behaved like a loving pet. He was not playful, but he was obedient and protective. It was not long before they crossed paths with a pack of hyena. These cunning, strategic creatures were known for traveling and attacking in packs and for being relentless, especially if they felt they had the advantage. The massive lion moved in front of Simon. He let out a loud, vicious roar that caused most of the hyenas to back up. However, they regrouped and slowly approached.

The massive lion roared once more, and the entire pack of hyena turned and ran in all different directions. In the blink of an eye, eight lions raced past Simon and his new bodyguard. Three other lions moved in closer to Simon and the alpha male, and they protected him on all sides. The lions chased the hyenas away. They did not chase to frighten. They chased to kill and kill they did with unforgiving ferociousness.

Simon watched with excitement and enthusiasm. He had seen lions hunt from a distance, but not while standing right in the middle of it. He realized something startling. He realized why his view was so exciting and so explicit. He could see every single lion and every single hyena all at the same time. But how could that be? They were not all in one line of sight. The hyena scattered in different directions and the lions chased each one. He noticed something different about the behavior of the lions. His enthusiasm turned into curiosity as he observed more intently.

The lions were not just killing the hyena in the spirit of protection. They were viciously and uncharacteristically ripping them apart. They were attacking with a savageness as he had never seen. They were only this vicious when protecting their young. The lions were being extremely cruel. Simon swore it was a personal vendetta.

The smaller animals were easily overpowered by the much larger and merciless lions. Simon carefully observed one instance in which two lions grabbed the same hyena and began to play tug-of-war. One lion had a tight grip on the throat of the doomed creature, while the other had a hindquarter in its jaws. The poor creature was ripped in half. The body exploded, and guts and intestine and every other organ flew in all directions. Blood spattered the face of both lions, and they barely flinched. What was left of the carcass dropped from their jaws, and they were soon chasing another hyena.

One swipe from the paw of another huge beast and a hyena was slowed enough for the lion to finish it off. Simon witnessed a lion bite a hyena behind its head and broke its neck. He could hear the breaking of bones from where he stood. The huge beast then shook the dead hyena like a rag doll. The head of the dead creature fell to the ground, and the lion continued to shake what was left of the body. A few of the hyenas became a meal for some of the lions. Simon was amazed. Each hyena was caught and killed. Not one of them survived.

The alpha male and the other three lions waited patiently as the hungry lions consumed their meal. When they were finished, they got back into formation as if they had done this before. The three lions that had moved in close to protect Simon stayed in their positions. The alpha male slowly walked forward, and Simon and the lions continued their journey.

As they walked, Simon became lost in thought again. His mind raced a million miles a minute. While he was trying to take in and comprehend all that had happened over the last few days, his head was filling with facts and information about Jesus and His message. He was in a mental duel with himself. The more he tried to figure out why everything was happening and why it was happening to him, the more information he received about Christ. Something was telling him to relax and to let go, to just believe and have faith. He knew this was the work of Jesus, but he kept wondering why him. One thing he had learned from his quick acquisition of knowledge was that obedience was paramount. He decided to do just that. He stopped questioning and started accepting all that was happening to him.

They walked for days, stopping only for the lions to feed, drink, and relieve themselves. They stopped at nightfall to rest. Simon lied down each night, but he very seldom slept. His new friends surrounded him at all times, and at least two of them stayed up and alert during the night. Not only did Simon have newly acquired knowledge, but he had new energy and enthusiasm. He seemed to never tire or get hungry. He had not eaten since he finished the last of his meat days earlier, and yet he was not hungry.

He continued to wonder what work Jesus had for him. He wasn't sure what it was, but he was sure he was being prepared for it. He could feel his transition as plainly as he could feel the ground on which he was lying. He could feel it in his mind and body. He swore that he could even feel it in his soul. He had changed from a man who hardly ever prayed to one who felt lonely and helpless without it.

Simon began to wonder which of the twelve he would be most like. Would he doubt like Thomas, or would he be fiery like Peter? Would he be loved as much as John, or would he be hated more than Judas? Before he could finish this line of thinking, he wondered how he knew so much about the disciples of Jesus. He had never met any of them. He saw a few of them at the crucifixion. However, at that time, he did not know who they were. He did not ponder on this for long because he knew the answer. Perplexed, yet content, he gazed up at the stars until the morning light hid their brightness.

The next day he parted ways with his new friends. He had come to the end of the bush and was not far from home. He could not wait to see his sons, even though he knew his visit would be short-lived. He wanted to see his sons grow into strong young men, but he knew that was not part of his destiny. In his wisdom, Jesus knew the longer Simon stayed around his family, the harder it would be for him to leave. Simon knew this as well, and he would be obedient. He prayed that the work Jesus had for him would not cause him to forget his family.

Simon had another day of walking before he would reach his home. His sons, Rufus and Alexander, were a day away. He could cut five or six hours from his time if he quickened his pace without stopping. Maybe he should slow down and take his time. The sooner he arrived, the sooner he would have to leave. He struggled with this dilemma at least a dozen times over the last few days. Just as he could feel the mental and physical change of his body, he could feel the internal struggle of having to leave his kids become less and less daunting. The closer he got to his homeland, the more he focused on the newly acquired knowledge that was constantly filling his head and why Jesus had chosen him. He began to wonder if helping the suffering Jesus on His crucifixion walk was his choice or if meeting the Messiah was predestined.

CHAPTER 2

THE HOME COMING

Simon had almost reached his destination. He could see his house. There were so many things going through his mind that he was having trouble concentrating. He had plenty of questions but no answers. He was frustrated. Everything had happened so quickly. During his walk with the lions, he discovered that Jesus had given him a lot of power, but how should his new abilities be used? Why did he even need them to do what Jesus wanted him to do? Like the rest of his newly acquired knowledge, the answer suddenly came to him. He concluded that Jesus is the answer. That's it; Jesus is the answer! Jesus wanted people to know about Him, to believe and trust Him. No, that's not it, at least not the full reason. His work was not only to introduce people to Jesus but to encourage, strengthen, and ignite their faith, to heal their despair, and to keep hope alive through the promises of Jesus.

His assignment was clear to him now. The clarity was a bit frightening because this was a lifelong commitment. Something about the length of the assignment concerned him, but he couldn't put his finger on it. He didn't mind serving Jesus until his death. What he would learn later was that he would be serving Jesus for hundreds of years.

Simon put this out of his head for now. He would think about it later. He could see his two sons, and he focused on them. He had been gone a few weeks, but it seemed like it had been much longer. He knew that Rufus and Alexander would remember their father, but the enemy tried to convince him otherwise. The good thing was that the enemy seemed to have less and less influence over him with each passing minute, but he was still persistent, still convincing, and still evil.

Simon stopped about thirty yards from his sons. He watched them and observed how active and how curious they were. He saw how well they played with each other and how close they appeared to be. They were two innocent boys full of energy and adventure. There were so many things he wanted to know about their future, and he was afraid that he would never know. Who would they pray to? Would they pray at all? What would they remember about their father?

He noticed that the boys had stopped playing and were staring at him. He made eye contact with them. Then Simon slowly walked toward them. After he had taken a few steps, both boys simultaneously broke out in a full run toward him. "Poppa, Poppa!" they yelled. Just hearing and seeing them melted Simon's heart. He bent down with his arms stretched out wide. He picked up both boys and twirled them around in a circle. They giggled and screamed, enjoying every second of it.

"How are my two, favorite people in the whole world?" asked Simon, as he gently set them down?

"Have you seen the whole world?" asked Alexander enthusiastically.

Simon laughed and roughed up his son's hair. "Not yet I haven't. What have you two guys been up to since I've been away?"

"We've been good," insisted Rufus in a very unconvincing manner.

"We'll see about that. Where is your mother?"

"Poppa, your hands are red," said Rufus. "Are they bleeding? Do they hurt?"

"No, they are not bleeding, and no, they do not hurt."

"Poppa, you need to wash your hands," insisted Alexander.

"Yeah, Poppa, wash your hands," said Rufus.

"My hands are red, but they are clean. Besides, it would take a long time for this red color to wear off. You boys will just have to get used to it. Where is your mother?"

"She's in there," said a very talkative Rufus, pointing to the house, "but she's busy. Don't you want to stay out here and play with us?"

"Of course, I do, but I haven't seen your mother in a long time either. I want to see her too. I will be back out here to play with both of you. It won't be too long. I promise."

"Momma's busy," said Alexander. She doesn't have time to play."

"She's not too busy for Daddy."

"Uh-huh," said Rufus, "she made us come out here because she said she was busy."

"What's keeping her so busy?" asked Simon.

"I don't know; she said she's got stuff to do."

"Yeah, she's got stuff to do," agreed Alexander, "so you can stay out here with us."

"Let me go see what she's doing. Maybe I can help her," insisted Simon. "Don't worry; I'll be back out here to play with you guys."

"Okay," said a smiling Rufus, "but hurry up."

"Yeah, hurry up," repeated Alexander.

Simon turned and started walking toward the house when he saw Bree standing a couple of steps from the doorway. She was smiling as she had watched him playing and talking with their children. Simon smiled at his wife. She was as attractive as ever.

"I couldn't see the boys, so I thought I should step out here and make sure they were okay. I had no idea you were back. What a wonderful surprise."

"They are better than okay," said Simon. "They are wonderful. You, my queen, are lovelier than ever, and I have missed you so much."

"I have missed you too, my king. Come inside and let me show you how much."

"We will make up for lost time, but not now. I do not want Rufus and Alexander to interrupt my time with my wife, so I will give them their time now. I will play with them and get them good and tired. When they fall asleep tonight, the king and his queen will become one."

"So, what is the story behind those bloody hands? I heard the boys ask you about them. Is that your blood? Are you sure you're okay?"

"No, it's not my blood, and yes, I am fine. I will tell you all about it later tonight. Let me get back to the boys for now, and we will have time together tonight.

"Don't let the boys tire you out too much."

"You do not have to be concerned with that," said Simon laughing. As he walked away, Bree watched them for a few moments before going back into the house.

"You two are in for it," teased Simon as he walked back toward his sons. They both ran to him, jumped on him, and punched him. Simon fell down in the grass as if they had knocked him down. They laughed and giggled and jumped all over him. Simon rolled on top of them and gently punched them in return. He then shoved Alexander to one side and pushed Rufus in the opposite direction. They ran back to him, more excited and aggressive than ever.

As Simon got on his knees, Rufus jumped on his back and held him around the neck. Alexander jumped on top of Rufus. Simon reached back over his head and grabbed Alexander with his right hand and held him out in front of him like a rag doll. As he rose to his feet, Rufus held on for dear life. He then grabbed Alexander by his ankles and held him upside down. As he swung Alexander around, both boys laughed uncontrollably.

"Do me next, Poppa; do me!" shouted Rufus.

Simon released his right hand and held Alexander by the ankle with only his left hand. He then reached down behind him and grabbed the right ankle of Rufus. As he slowly lifted Rufus's leg into the air, Rufus held on tight to Simon's neck. When he extended his arm straight up to its full length, Rufus finally released his grip. Instead of holding them straight in front of him, Simon held his arms out from his side and spun around in a circle.

Rufus and Alexander were having the time of their lives. They were full of energy and excitement, and there was no sign of them tiring anytime soon. Simon continued to play and wrestle with them for about two hours. They ran and chased each other and played all kinds of games. He enjoyed every minute of it, more than the boys would ever know. He knew he would have to leave them soon, and he wanted to leave them with good memories of the time they had with their father. Then he remembered the promise of Jesus: that his sons would remember him.

"Ok fellas, hold up. It's getting late, and you haven't eaten your dinner yet."

"We're not hungry, Poppa. We want to play some more," said Rufus.

"Yeah, we want to play some more," repeated Alexander.

"I tell you what," said Simon, "we will compromise."

"What is compromise?" asked Alexander.

"It means that both of you and I will agree on something. You don't have to go in and eat your dinner just yet if you walk around with me for a little while. Is that a deal?"

"I want to play," said Alexander.

"Me too," said Rufus.

"We have played enough for today. You either go in now and eat your dinner and then get ready for bed, or we walk around a little first. Which one will it be?"

"Okay, okay, we will walk with you," said Rufus. "Where are we going?"

"Nowhere in particular; I just want to see what's been going on with you two since I have been gone and talk to you about a couple of things."

Simon, Rufus, and Alexander walked around for an hour, talking about virtually everything. He asked them about their friends and their schooling and told them about their culture and the history of Cyrene. Simon made sure they remembered the rules that he and their mother had put in place to keep them out of harm's way. He even tested them on some of the pointers he had taught them about hunting. This saddened him because he realized right then that he would never take them hunting. He didn't let his sons see the hurt he was feeling at that moment. It was getting dark, so he tested them on their sense of direction. He showed them different landscapes and scenery and star patterns in the sky to remember. He wanted to make sure they could find their way home if they ever got lost.

Finally, Simon talked to them about Jesus. He eased into the conversation to keep from overwhelming them. He asked Rufus and Alexander where they thought people came from? Who made the grass grow and the rain fall? Why didn't the stars fall from the sky? They knew of the chief priest, but did they know who he prayed to.

As much as Simon tried not to overwhelm his children, he was doing exactly that. He could see the confusion and looks of bewilderment on their faces. He realized that his sons had not yet been taught about Jesus. Up until this moment in their young lives, the religious knowledge of his sons was tribal and primitive. He changed that immediately. There was so much he wanted to tell them about Jesus, but he knew their young minds could comprehend only so much at this time. He made a mental note to make sure that his sons would be brought up in Christ in his absence. He knew how it would be done. Tomorrow, he would have a long talk with father Zureeba, the chief priest. For now, he made sure they remembered the name Jesus, and he made his sons promise to learn all they could about Him.

Simon knew the knowledge he had of Jesus came through divine intervention and was far more complete than most anyone, except His disciples and a few others whom Jesus had handpicked. He would later learn that a lot of his divine knowledge of Scripture had not yet been recorded. Jesus had just been crucified a week earlier, and He was not widely known at this point. Yes, His fame had spread throughout the region, but He was thought more of as a charlatan than anything else. Simon wanted to make sure his sons knew and worshiped Jesus as the son of God.

Rufus and Alexander had worked up a healthy appetite. As soon as they arrived home, both boys followed their nose to the meal their mom had prepared for them. Bree made them wash their hands in the wash bowl before they sat down at the table. Simon washed his hands as well, but they were still blood red. The boys were about to start eating their dinner when Simon stopped them. They all turned to him with perplexed looks on their faces.

"Do you remember what I was telling you about Jesus?" Simon asked.

"Yes, poppa," said Rufus.

"Well, Jesus would really appreciate it if we thanked Him for providing this meal for us. Put your hands together in a praying position, bow your heads, and repeat after me."

The boys looked confused, but they obeyed his instructions. Bree also did as he had asked because she knew her husband would explain this to her later. In their culture, women did not have much authority and certainly had none over men. Simon's wife never questioned or challenged his decisions because it was not her place to do so. However, she was grateful that her husband did not treat her like a piece of property. He always explained things to her or talked things over with her to get her opinion on important matters. She knew that he felt strongly about Jesus and his teachings. She had heard rumors about Jesus, as had most of the citizens of Cyrene, but she and Simon had spoken about Him only in passing. Something must have happened to influence his opinion of Jesus. She wondered if his red hands had anything to do with it.

As Simon prayed, his family repeated after him. He first praised and thanked God for making salvation possible through Jesus. He then asked God to forgive him and his family for their sins and thanked God for the mercy He had shown them. He thanked God for His love and the many blessings God had bestowed on him and his family. Lastly, he thanked God for the meal that had been prepared and prayed for guidance and direction in everything they did.

He ended his prayer by saying amen and told his family that they could start eating. He was surprised but very pleased that his boys asked him many questions about his prayer. He thought they were being unusually obedient to get through it so that they could hurry up and start eating, but obviously, they had been paying attention to every word. They asked him about salvation and what Jesus had to do with it. They asked about sin, mercy, and blessings and about what amen means. Simon was in awe and thanked Jesus for their curiosity. He answered their questions in a way in which they could understand and urged them to learn as much as they could about Jesus.

Bree was also in awe, but for a different reason. She was used to her boys asking a lot of questions, but she was learning as they were. She was fascinated by the depth of knowledge Simon had displayed about Jesus. He spoke with such confidence, clarity, and enthusiasm as if he had studied Jesus all his life. She and Simon both recognized that Rufus and Alexander appeared to be confused about some of the information he had shared with them. She was confused about some of it as well. Simon purposely described Jesus in such a fascinating way that they would have additional questions about Him.

The meal and the explanation of the prayer ended simultaneously. Simon planned it that way. He was truly thankful that his boys were genuinely interested in what he was telling them. He had a short period of time to influence them as much as he could, and he did not want to waste a minute of it. However, he did not want to overload them with information to the point of boredom or rejection. Rufus had a few more questions he wanted to ask after finishing his meal, but Simon told him he would talk to him more about Jesus after a good night's sleep. He told them it was getting late, and he would allow them to stay up another hour before they had to turn in for the night. He wanted to keep them curious, encouraging them to ask questions and learn about Jesus.

The boys did not need their normal coaxing to go to bed. The excitement of their father being home coupled with the energy they exerted playing with him had worn them out. They were both fast asleep within minutes of their heads hitting their pillows. Simon beamed with pride as he tucked his boys in. His family was healthy, beautiful, and genuinely interested in Jesus Christ. As proud and as happy as he was at that moment, a little loneliness started to creep into his heart. Though it was a few days away, he was dreading the moment when he would have to leave his family. He suppressed those thoughts as he went to be with his wife.

As much as Bree wanted to be with her husband, Simon's red hands spooked her a little. She had married a warrior and had seen bloody hands many times after a successful hunt. However, he was always able to wash the blood off, and they never looked as bright and alive as his hands looked now. Simon convinced his wife that she had nothing to be concerned about, and he promised to tell her the full story regarding his bloody hands.

He and Bree snuggled together. It was their time now, and they made the most of it. They held each other all night long. They enjoyed each other with a passion that most people only dreamt about. They were inseparable that night. They laid in each other's arms for a long time before either one of them said anything. Bree finally broke the silence.

"What's on your mind, my king?"

"Just thinking about what a beautiful family I have and how blessed I am."

"You're a different man since you came back, my love; not in a bad way, just different."

"How am I different?"

"You mean besides the red hands?"

"Yes, besides the red hands."

"There is a peace about you that I can't describe. Though you have always been a loving father and an attentive husband, you seem to be even more caring and more loving than ever. You still have a very authoritative presence, but I don't detect the warrior spirit as much. You talk quite a bit about the man called Jesus, and I think He had something to do with the change in you. Did you meet Him on your journey?"

"Yes, I met Him, and now is as good a time as any to tell you all about it."

Simon started telling his wife all about his encounter with Jesus. He explained how he had followed the crowd to see what was about to take place. He told Bree how some were calling for His death, while others were begging for His life. He told her about the two men carrying crosses, the beaten and bleeding Jesus, the crucifixion, and his overwhelming urge to help Jesus.

"The blood of Jesus is on your hands?" she asked.

"Yes," confirmed Simon.

He went on to describe how he felt when he and Jesus had made eye contact. He explained how Jesus thanked him and talked to him without opening His mouth. He also told Bree about the question Jesus asked him: Was he ready to go to work? Simon shared with Bree everything that happened to him on his journey home. He explained the lions protecting him and escorting him through the bush. He told her about the things he seemed to know that he never knew before and how he could read people's thoughts at times. He explained to her that until a day or so ago he wasn't sure what work Jesus had for him. Now he knew what it was, and he shared his thoughts with her.

Tears came to her eyes when she learned that her husband would have to leave soon and that she would probably never see him again. He comforted her as much as he could, but Bree did not fully understand why he was being asked to leave his family. She wanted

24

him to stay home with her to help her raise their sons. She wanted him there for herself. She was willing to share her husband with Jesus as long as he could remain in Cyrene. Even if he couldn't stay, why couldn't she and the boys go with him? He tried to explain it to her, but she was too emotional at that time and could only focus on him leaving, never to return.

Simon wiped the tears from her eyes and held her tighter. He knew that there was nothing he could say now to comfort her, but he was confident that she would understand once she had established a personal relationship with Christ. He apologized to her for having to leave in a couple of days, but he made her promise him that she would learn as much about Jesus and His teachings as she could. She promised to make sure their boys learned about Jesus as well.

They laid in each other's arms the rest of the night without speaking a word. Bree tried to be strong, but she couldn't stop the tears from flowing.

CHAPTER 3

TIME TO SERVE

S imon's time had come; it was time for him to leave his beloved family and city. The last twenty-four hours had been very sad and very painful. He did not tell his boys that he would never see them again. He told them that he had to leave again on one of his trips. Rufus sensed something was not right by his father's demeanor and body language. Simon had talked to his boys quite a bit about Jesus over the last two days, and Alexander asked his father if he was going to meet Jesus. Simon answered Alexander by saying he would be doing some work for Jesus. That answer caused Rufus to think that his father would be gone longer than usual.

Bree was having a hard time hiding her emotions from her children, especially as the time drew closer for Simon to leave. She had been crying almost continuously. This was the second clue that convinced Rufus that something wasn't right. Every time his father talked about his journey, his mother would shed a few tears, which she had never done in the past. On a couple of occasions, she left the room to keep her sons from seeing her cry.

Bree struggled with believing in Simon's God. It's not that she didn't want to. She was just having a hard time understanding how someone so full of love, as Simon had described Jesus, could cause them so much pain. She never told her husband how much she resented his God for taking him away from them, but Simon knew.

His faith had assured him that she would not feel that way for long.

Bree found it more difficult than usual to say goodbye, but she summoned the strength to get through it without appearing distraught. She kissed Simon and embraced him right before he left.

She watched him leave as Rufus and Alexander followed him out. Simon played with his sons and talked to them as they walked. He made them promise him that they would never forget what he had taught them about Jesus. Bree watched from a window. The boys loved their father so much that she did not have the heart to tell them that they would never see him again. She knew that conversation would come far too soon, and she would never be ready for it.

She watched as Simon came to a stop about fifty yards away. He bent down and hugged both of his sons for a long time. He struggled to keep his composure, but he stayed strong for their sake. He tried his best to treat this departure like the many others they had been through. The boys, who would be teenagers in a few years, were accustomed to their father leaving every so often. However, this departure was harder than the others. He was usually home much longer between trips. He had been home only a few days and was now heading back out.

After the long hugs, Simon said goodbye and told his boys to go back to the house and take care of their mother. They didn't want to leave their father just yet; they procrastinated, but they were obedient. Simon told them that he loved them and that he would be thinking about them. Rufus and Alexander told their father that they loved him too and told him to hurry back. Simon watched them as they slowly walked back to the house, turning around often, and waving to their father. Simon stood there for a while getting a last glimpse of his sons and waving each time they waved. The last time they turned to wave, Simon had his back to them and was on his way. With their heads down, Rufus and Alexander slowly walked home.

Jesus promised Simon that He would take care of his family and comfort them. Simon believed it without a doubt. He was at peace now about having to leave his family. He attributed that peace to Jesus.

Simon knew that if Jesus had done that for him, He would keep His promise and do it for his family also.

As confident as he was that his family would be safe, Simon could not help but think about his sons. His faith was strong and would get stronger, but young boys need their father. Of course, he thought about his wife as well. Women had no authority and could not own property. His oldest son could become heir to the property when he was declared dead, but any man who had the inclination to do so could claim Bree and the property as his own. Anyone who believed otherwise would have to fight the claimant, and this was a fight to the death. His sons were not old enough or skilled enough for such a battle, but he knew that Rufus would attempt to protect his mother if a situation presented itself.

These things consumed Simon's thoughts as he walked. He knew his service would last a long time, but he did not know exactly how long. He knew he would soon be busy with the work that Jesus had for him, and he hoped he would never forget about his family. He prayed to Jesus and asked Him to never allow the memories of his family to be taken from him. Jesus reminded him that worrying about his family was the opposite of faith. He convinced himself that he was not worrying about his family, simply thinking about them.

Simon had been walking for a few hours when his first challenge presented itself. He came upon a small village, and the scene was familiar to him. There was a group of people huddled around someone. He noticed that a small child appeared to be ill or injured. He walked in the direction of the child to better determine what was going on and to see if he could help.

"Continue your journey and do not help the child."

Simon stopped in his tracks. He wondered if he had heard what he thought he had heard. His heart dropped as a woman cried over a female child who had now lost consciousness.

"I can help her. I want to help her. Why can't I help her?" he whispered.

"Her death will accomplish the will of the Father far more so than her life, and she will live in the presence of the Father throughout eternity."

"That can't be true," said Simon, as he continued walking toward the girl.

"Continue your journey and do not attempt to help the child."

At that moment, Simon's desire to help a child took priority over his desire to be obedient to Jesus. A woman, who Simon assumed was the child's mother, had picked up the child and was crying over her. Though unconscious, the child gasped for air in a struggle to breathe. A small group of people surrounded the woman to comfort her. He wondered why everyone was crying and mourning and why no one was trying to help. When he got closer, he saw a wound on the child's leg, which was swollen and stained with blood. The child had been bitten by a poisonous snake, and there was no antidote.

"Let me have her," Simon said. "I can help her."

They did not understand what Simon wanted. He was a stranger to them, and they did not trust him. They backed away from him, and a few of them positioned themselves between Simon and the woman. They treated him as if he meant to do the child harm. Simon did not understand. He was sure that he could speak to them in their language, which wasn't much different from his, but they did not understand him. They would not let him get near the child.

Simon kept his distance. He could see that he was scaring them. He puts his hands together as if he was praying and begged them to give him the child. Though they worshiped different gods, they knew the symbol for prayer. Simon kept asking as they talked among themselves.

The woman with the child forced her way between the others and walked up to Simon. She gently handed her daughter over to him. Simon took the little girl and cradled her in his arms. He nodded softly to the woman, assuring her that she had done the right thing. As he held the child, he gently rubbed the swollen leg. They did not know what Simon was saying as he prayed to Jesus.

Suddenly he felt alone. He could not feel the presence of Jesus. He begged Jesus to help the child, but his request was denied. He could not tell if the child was breathing. She was lying so still and lifeless. He felt for a heartbeat but could not locate one. Tears rolled down his cheeks as he looked up at the child's mother, who collapsed to her knees and sobbed uncontrollably. Two of the bystanders helped the woman to her feet as a third woman took the child from Simon and gave him a nasty look.

Simon wiped the tears from his face as he tried to figure out why he couldn't help the child. He was sure that he could. They couldn't even understand him, yet the mother trusted him with her child. He felt guilty for giving them false hope. Had the power that had been given to him been taken away? He had helped others. Why didn't Jesus help him save the child?

You were instructed to continue your journey and not attempt to help the child.

"Why did you not allow me to heal the child?" asked Simon. "I wasn't even able to communicate with them. I don't understand why an innocent child had to die."

"I told you that the death of the child will advance the Father's kingdom far more than her life. You were disobedient. You have a good heart, Simon, which is why you were selected, but to serve Me, you must be obedient. You have no authority outside of Me."

"Help me to understand, Lord! This is a terrible feeling that I never want to experience again."

"You are a compassionate man, Simon, and you will always want to help alleviate the pain of others. However, you must have faith and trust and believe that I know what is best. Your faith is proven through your obedience. You must be obedient, even when you disagree or don't understand."

"The idol gods that this small village worships are illusions that hinder their salvation. The death of the child will cause them to doubt their gods and will lead them to Me. This village will be destroyed by a disaster in a couple of years. No one will survive it. If the child had lived, they would have rejected the gospel, which will be preached to them in a few months. Since the child died, they will listen and be

more receptive to the gospel and become believers. The young child has already been granted eternal life in the presence of the Father. Those who reject the gospel will be doomed to eternal damnation. It is better to lose a child now and save a village than to save a child and lose a village. Satan used your compassion, which can be a weakness, to influence you. The enemy also is aware of the future disaster of this village. He knows that if the child had lived, the inhabitants of the village faced eternal death."

Simon understood, but it was a hard lesson for him to learn. He quietly continued on his way. He could not help but think of his own children. He hoped that someone would be able to help his boys if they were ever in distress. A tear rolled down his cheek. He quickly wiped his face and increased his pace.

Now he understood that the will of the Father was inevitable. He knew that Jesus is the only way to the Father. However, he never thought he would have to allow a child to die. Simon was starting to realize how serious the spreading of the gospel was. This was a hard but necessary lesson to learn.

As he continued his journey, he had no idea where he was going. He knew the land but not his destination. He had been instructed to travel in this direction, and so he did. Jesus directed his path. If he came to a fork in the road, he was told which path to take.

As he walked, he was feeling very vulnerable. He would never forget the face of the suffering child. He would not forget the tears running down the faces of those who tried to help her. It would be a while before the sobs of agony and despair stopped haunting him. He had never felt so powerful and so helpless at the same time. At that particular moment, an unexplainable force knocked Simon to his knees. This fearless warrior couldn't keep the tears from flowing.

Jesus allowed Simon time to grieve. This was a learning experience for him and a very important one. He had just learned, the hard way, that his desire to help must never take priority over his obedience to Christ. He learned that our temporary comfort is not as important as our eternal home. Simon did not grieve long. He was soon on his way.

Simon learned a lot as he traveled around the world for centuries on end. However, nothing that he learned would compare to the harsh lesson of obedience he learned from having to watch a child die. He was sure that would be something he would never forget. He had met a lot of people and seen a lot of things through his travels. He realized that no matter where he went, and how different people may look, they were all basically the same.

Yes, they spoke differently, dressed differently, and had different cultures and mannerisms but they were all focused on the family unit. They all cherished and wanted to protect and provide for their families. How this was done was often different, but it was always a top priority. Simon was amazed how easily this was forgotten when people came across others of different ethnic backgrounds and different cultures. He never understood why there was almost an immediate feeling of distrust and often hatred, when people of different skin colors, or ethnic origins, or languages met one another. This became more evident and more troubling as the earth became more populated. Simon would learn that this troubling behavior would escalate into inhumane treatment toward each other.

CHAPTER 4

TROUBLED TIMES

Guinea, West Africa – 1602

Simon had now fully accepted his calling without question. He had witnessed and had acted on behalf of Jesus in thousands of situations. He had traveled the world for hundreds of years and had not aged a day. The enemies of Christ had threatened him thousands of times, but no weapon sent against him was successful. He had performed miracles beyond explanation and had wielded power beyond comprehension, yet he was humbler than he had ever been. He knew that he had no power without Jesus. Everything that he had accomplished, every place he had been, and every Scripture he had uttered was per the instruction of his Lord. He was slowly becoming the perfect servant.

However, there were times when Simon disagreed with Jesus and wanted to act contrary to what he was being told. He never forgot about the little girl who died when he first started on this journey; the little girl he knew he could have helped. However, that incident taught him some valuable lessons. Satan was trying to put doubt in his mind, trying to cause division between him and Christ. He saw how those villagers turned from their idol gods and searched for a god that could save their children. He remembered how they embraced Jesus when they were introduced to Him. He had witnessed the destruction of that small village. He knew that small colony would live forever with Jesus.

Simon was much more successful in his self-denial and obedience after that day, though his worldly desire to do things his way still surfaced from time to time.

A loud, painful, agonizing scream caused Simon to stop in his tracks. He was traveling through a hilly area, and the terrifying sound was a couple of hundred yards below him. He walked faster, searching for the origin of the scream. The closer he got to its source, the more convinced he became that a battle was taking place. As a warrior, he knew that sound very well. As he approached a clearing, Simon could clearly see what was taking place about eighty yards beneath him.

"Observe only, do not interfere, and make sure your presence is not discovered."

"What am I witnessing, my Lord?"

"You're witnessing the single largest event that will glorify the Father and magnify the Son for many centuries to come. Observe only!"

Simon watched the foreigners in the funny clothing converge on a small village. They beat, captured, and shackled those who called this land home. This was indeed a battle, a very unfair and cruel one. There were many foreigners, and they surrounded the village. This battle was different from the ones he had been involved in or any that he had witnessed. These men were not looting the village. They were not protecting their own or fending off intruders. He watched with intense interest as the children cried because their parents were being beaten and dragged off. The children were carried off as well.

Simon watched in amazement. His eyes widened as he realized what was taking place. He watched the foreigners work with speed and efficiency. The natives tried to fight back with no success.

"My Lord," whispered Simon with grave concern.

"It is exactly what you think it is. This is a manhunt. Your people are being collected. They will be enslaved for centuries. When their institutional slavery ends, they will continue to be mistreated and taken advantage of until I return. Their suffering will turn them to Me, and I will hear their cry. I will bless them amid their turmoil. Your people honor the Father more than any other, and they have

many treasures stored up for them in heaven."

Though Simon's travels had taken him all over the world, he had never witnessed anything like what he was witnessing at that moment. The weapons of the foreigners were much more advanced than anything he had seen. Their swords were longer, sharper, and stronger. They had handheld machines that hurled projectiles at such speed and force that they pierced the body and knocked you off your feet. They used large, strong nets to trap their captives as if they were catching fish. Though only a few of the natives were killed, the foreigners acted with such cruelty and malice that you would think it was personal. However, he could tell that it was business as usual by the precision in which they worked. This was not the first village they had raided.

The captives were rounded up and herded off. They were shackled at the ankles and led away. Simon looked off in the distance and saw a large ship sitting about a hundred yards offshore. The captives were being taken to the coast and placed in small boats that took them to the large ship.

He witnessed a sight that disturbed him. He was about to act but was stopped by Jesus.

"Stay put my friend and observe. I know this is hard for you to watch, but it must be allowed to take place. Do not interfere."

One of the boats capsized. The two foreigners onboard swam to another boat while the chained captives flailed for their lives. They had no chance as they began to sink. Two of the captives were a woman and her child. The foreigners did not lift a finger to attempt a rescue, but they retrieved the small boat as they continued toward the large ship. Egypt cannot have been this bad, thought Simon.

He witnessed pain, suffering, and death brought about because of disobedience. The men were beaten, and the children threatened as the women watched and begged for mercy. The women allowed themselves to be abused to protect their men and their children. Simon watched for about an hour until every last man, woman, and child in the village had been taken to the big ship.

Simon became very angry. He could not remember the last time he was so upset. In fact, he didn't think he had ever been as angry as he was then. To make things worse, the men were returning. Seven or eight small boatloads of them were returning to the shore. The foreigners secured their boats and marched down the shore headed south. He knew of a similar village that was a few miles up the coast, and he was sure that these foreigners knew it as well. Simon felt that he must stop this manhunt of his people, and he headed downhill in the direction of the foreigners.

"Stop! Do not interfere! Your people will be restored and blessed beyond anything they can imagine. One day, one of your countrymen will be considered the most powerful man in the world, and no race will be closer to the Father than yours. Head east and do not turn back."

Simon stopped as he was instructed. He stood still for what seemed like an eternity. He had an internal conflict going on inside of him; one like he had never experienced before. He knew that he should be obedient, but he felt an obligation to help his people. He trusted Jesus with all his heart, but this was so very painful to watch. He was born and trained to be a warrior. He was raised to love and protect his people, even at the cost of his own life. Though the villagers were not blood relatives or even of the same tribe, he considered them his people, and they did nothing to deserve the treatment he had just witnessed. His hands began to glow with an intensity he had not experienced. He could feel a great power surge through his body, and his hands felt as if they were about to explode. Then, just as suddenly as his hands began to glow, they stopped, and with great anguish, Simon turned and walked away with a heavy heart.

November 1938 – Nazi Germany

After viewing the enslavement of his people, without being allowed to help, Simon left his homeland and headed back to Europe, per the instructions of Jesus. Europe and Africa had a history of conflict based on religion, and that was what Jesus wanted Simon to know. He had been in Europe the last five hundred years and witnessed the Crusades; religious wars between the Christians and the Muslims. Just when he thought man might be tired of fighting, he visited his homeland and witnessed a different type of battle—a fight for freedom. His return trip to Europe centuries later was not much better. He was there for only a short period when another religious war took place. It would be known as the Thirty Years' War and pitted the Protestants against the Catholics. It started out as a religious war but escalated into a political power struggle between some of the European powers. The Thirty Years' War was responsible for the death of over eight million people, including twenty percent of the German population.

Three hundred years had passed, and Simon found himself back in Europe. World War I, one of the costliest wars in European history, was taking place. Millions of lives were lost. Germany was right in the middle of it and suffered the plight of being on the losing side, which left a bad taste in the mouth of a young Hitler who would soon rise to power.

Less than twenty years later Simon slowly walked around a burning city. Synagogues were burning. Piles of religious books were burning. Jewish artifacts were burning. Some personal residences were burning. Civility and compassion were not present. Half of the citizens were attacking and killing the other half. People were beaten and killed, and mercy was nowhere to be found. It appeared to be a civil war, but the victims were offering very little resistance. Those who did paid for it with their lives.

Simon was not visible to anyone and walked freely wherever he chose. He had been instructed to observe only and did not think of interfering, until he saw children being treated as badly as the adults. He could not stand to see a child being mistreated or in pain without wanting to help. He stopped himself from aiding a young boy who was being dragged through the street by his hair. He would always remember that one time when he attempted to help a child, and it did not go well. He would remain obedient and observe only, as he was instructed.

He continued to walk around what had become Nazi Germany. He could not believe his eyes. The atrocities he witnessed took him back a few centuries when his people were being collected like animals and forced into servitude. He would never forget the things he witnessed or how his people were mistreated in a foreign land. However, what he was witnessing now was a lot worse in many ways. His people were beaten, killed, and raped, which was the price they paid for resisting and being disobedient. These Germans were doing the same thing out of ignorance, ambition, and hatred. The only value the foreigners saw in his people were as laboring animals. The Germans saw no value in the Jews they were slaughtering.

Simon soon realized what was happening. He first thought the people had gone mad, attacking their neighbors for no reason. On further observation, he recognized that one ethnic group, the Jews, were being singled out. Those who were not immediately killed were confined like animals in concentration camps and killed later. The deaths were piling up by the minute.

"Jesus, these are Your people. Why are You allowing this to happen?"

"This experience is instrumental in fulfilling Scripture. Like your people, the Jews will be persecuted until I return. What you are witnessing now will be known as Kristallnacht, the Night of Broken Glass. My friend, this is just the beginning of what will be known as the Holocaust. You will see the Jews suffer much more than what you are witnessing now."

"I don't understand Lord! You mentioned Scripture. You have placed all Scripture in my head, but I don't recall reading about the Jews being treated like this."

"It is not so much the Scriptures pertaining to the suffering of my people, though there are many, but the Scriptures discussing the conversion of the Jews. What do you know about that?"

"I know there has been and will continue to be, discussions about

Jews having to convert to Christianity. Some say it has to happen before You return. Others argue it won't happen until after You return. Is the conversion necessary? If so, which argument is correct?"

"There are a lot of opinions on whether the conversion of the Jews is necessary or if it will happen at all. There are Scriptures regarding it, but most of them are somewhat veiled and only understood after a lot of study, meditation, and prayer. Tell me, my friend, what is the biggest difference between the religious belief of the Jews and those of the Christians?"

"Your people don't believe You are the son of the living God," said Simon.

"Correct, and those who do are referred to as Jewish Christians, converts, and a few other things. However, there is one Scripture that is very well known and repeated often that will clear up this question regarding the conversion of the Jews. It is simple and easy to understand."

"What Scripture is that?" asked Simon.

"Tell me what John 14:6 says."

"It is You talking to Your disciples. It says that You are the way and the truth and the life. No one comes to the Father except through You."

"What does that mean to you?"

"Lord, I see where You are going with this. You are the only path to the Father. The people who deny You as the son of the living God are denying God, Himself. Those people will never be in the Father's presence."

"I am the way, and there is no other. I am the truth, so listen to Me when I speak. There is no life outside of Me. It doesn't make a difference whether you are Jew or Gentile, rich or poor, a believer from birth or a convert, you must come through Me to meet the Father. That is simple enough for a child to understand. Your thoughts are correct, My friend."

"You're saying that the pain and suffering these Jews are enduring now will be a big factor in Jews accepting You in the future?"

"Yes! Always remember My friend, when things seem confusing and complicated, go to Scripture. The truth is in Scripture. No matter what man says

or how much knowledge he thinks he has, the truth is in Scripture."

"Yes, my Lord! Now that the question of conversion has been answered, will it happen before or after You return?

"The answer to that lies in Scripture as well. Search the book of Matthew, and you will find the answer."

Simon remained quiet for a few moments. He was recalling the entire book of Matthew to his memory. Verse by verse, chapter by chapter, he searched for the answer. Then he came to Matthew 23:39.

"Yes, that is the one I am referring to."

"Interesting," says Simon. "That verse is pretty clear. I don't understand why man continues to debate this issue."

"There are several reasons, but the two biggest are that man relies on his own intelligence and very seldom prays for understanding when reading Scripture. He usually reads just to get through it so that he can say he has read it. Simon of Cyrene, I want you to follow this attempt of Jewish extermination by the Germans until it comes to an end. There will be some opportunities for you to aid some of the distressed, and you will know when. However, observe only for the next year. You will be surprised what you learn about these atrocities."

Simon did as he was instructed. He learned a lot about human behavior, good and bad, from the German invasion of Western Europe. He never thought he would see anything as evil as the enslavement of his people. The Holocaust did not last as long as slavery, but it was just as evil. However, Simon was delighted to see some people help one another at the risk of their own lives. Some lost their lives while helping their neighbor, but they had no regrets. He called them warriors because he knew, given the opportunity, they would do it all over again.

Then it happened, but Simon had a hard time believing it. This must be what Jesus wanted him to learn. He watched a horrible scene in which a man died protecting his Jewish friend's children. The man's house was thoroughly searched, but the two children were well hidden under some floorboards under the kitchen table. Their parents had barely had enough time to hide the children before the Germans came busting into the house.

"Why are you protecting the Jewish pigs?" asked the German soldier. "You are like me. You should be helping me exterminate these pigs."

"I am nothing like you," said the man. Those were the last words he uttered before the German soldier shot him in the head.

"You are a weak Christian. You're right; you're nothing like me," said the soldier. He searched the house for a few minutes before exiting. The boy and girl stayed hidden until nightfall and all was quiet inside the house. The young boy slowly pushed away the floorboards, and then he helped his sister crawl out. They cried when they saw their father and his friend lying in their own blood. The boy grabbed his sister's hand and led her out of the house. They would soon find out that their mother had been killed also, but they would be okay. They would survive the Holocaust.

Simon was in total shock. The killings were horrible, but he could not get the German soldier's words out of his head; "You are like me." The soldier was not talking about his evil spirit. He was referring to his Christian faith. The German soldier professed to be a Christian. Simon prayed for knowledge and understanding and discovered that better than ninety percent of Germany at that time professed to be Christians. They were either Protestant or Catholic. These Germans were mostly confessed Christians who were killing Jews. Simon knew that the Jews were looked down on and despised by many after the death of Jesus, but he never imagined it would come to this. When he had an opportunity to observe and listen to Hitler, he realized there was more to the Holocaust atrocities than the death of Christ.

Simon watched millions of people die during the Holocaust, and they were not all Jews. The mentally and physically disabled, Polish, and Russian citizens, and anyone who attempted to halt the German invasion was forced to endure inhumane experiments and eventually death. The Scriptures taught him that God always had a remnant. The Holocaust taught him that everyone who claimed to be a Christian did not follow the teachings of Christ.

This seemed to be a recurring theme thought Simon; professed Christians who did not act anything like Christ. He remembered the Crusades, hundreds of years earlier, in which the Christians and the Muslims fought each other. Some people referred to it as The Holy Wars, but there was nothing holy about them. It seemed too often that blood was spilled in the name of religion and every religion that he had ever witnessed taught peace and love. How ironic was that?

The twentieth century was interesting to Simon. He wanted to help during the anti-apartheid and civil rights movements, but Jesus forbade it. It seemed that Nelson Mandela and Martin Luther King Jr. led the fight for their respective countries. However, Jesus told Simon that he would have plenty of opportunities to help aid in man's inhumanity to man. It was near the end of the twentieth century when Simon felt the most useful, and that continued right into the twenty-first century. He had assisted thousands of people by now, but his work started to seem more meaningful. He never complained one time about never receiving credit for his work. The Father and Son were always glorified, which is as it should be. He knew he was nothing without Them.

CHAPTER 5

THE ASSIGNMENT

Louisville, Kentucky - 2002

Feeling tired and thankful, Gwen sat on her couch watching the late news. She cradled Junior against her breast with her left arm and rested her right hand on his tiny chest. Her hand lay on top of the blanket that covered him. Junior had just fallen asleep. Gwen's eldest child, Rose, had gone to bed a couple of hours earlier. Junior was a sickly child, and this had not been a good day for him. Gwen was tired from having to tend to him all day, yet thankful that he was finally able to rest. She was glad it was Friday. This was the third day this week that she had to miss work to take care of him. She hated to leave her coworkers shorthanded so often, but she felt blessed that they, along with her supervisor, understood her situation and worked with her.

Her husband, John, was a high school basketball coach, and a pretty good one at that. He was named one of the best young coaches in the country by a national sports magazine. He was a disciplinarian, but his kids loved him. He was a player's coach and was like a father figure to his team. John helped them on and off the court. His teams were unselfish and played well as a unit. You could not play for him unless you did well in the classroom and respected your elders. He had a few players who were recruited by very successful division-one universities, and they did well once they got there.

John was taking a walk, which he often did after a tough loss or a

43

rough day. Here lately he had been walking quite a bit. While walking helped him to relax and helped to calm him, a candy bar was his celebratory food of choice. However, tonight was not such a night. He was having a hard time dealing with the fact that his only son, his name sake John Samuel Crenshaw Jr., was deathly ill. Every time Junior had an episode, John expected the worse. He thought he believed in God until his son was born sick. His faith was wavering, and he wasn't so sure anymore. He believed that a loving God would not allow his only son to die. Yet that was exactly what was happening. Every time he thought about it, he felt as if he was going to cry, but he never did. However, he did start to sweat, even in the cool night air. He removed his handkerchief from his hip pocket and wiped his face and neck. He looked at the initials on it, J. S. C. This was the name that he was so proud of, the name that he gave to his son.

As John placed the handkerchief back in his pocket, he thought about the fact that he and his wife could not have any more children. His namesake was fighting an incredible battle, and the odds were not in his favor. His mind started to drift, and he wondered if his son would ever play basketball or any sport for that matter. He hastened his pace but was careful not to overexert himself.

He wore a gold chain around his neck that supported a gold cross. The cross had a diamond on each end of it, with his initials engraved on the back. His grandmother had given it to him years earlier when he was a child. She told him to never take it off because it would protect him from evil. She explained that the day would come when he would fully understand what the cross represented, and on that day, he would not need the necklace anymore. On that day, the cross would be on the inside of him instead of the outside. As a child, John did not understand what his grandmother meant, but he loved her so much that he believed whatever she told him. His grandmother often spoke about Jesus to him, and he believed because she believed. Her faith was deeply rooted in Christ, just like his wife's. His grandmother had given him the cross at a young age, and John had worn it every day since, out of respect and in remembrance of her.

"Things could always be worse" was the phrase that came to Gwen's mind after watching a report about a local tragedy. A young man had been on his job for only three months before being severely injured in a factory explosion. A lot of people felt that the young man would have been better off had he died. He was burned over seventy-five percent of his body, and his skin looked as if it had melted. Roger Kelp lost one eye and his hearing, and he was paralyzed below the waist. His family and friends set up a fundraiser to pay for his medical expenses and the lifelong care he would need.

The part that broke Gwen's heart was that the young man had just confessed Christ as his Lord and Savior a month before his accident, and he had joined the Grief Ministry at his church. His father's death, a couple of years earlier, touched him in a way that made him want to help console people during tragic times. He didn't want anyone to go through the range of emotions that he had gone through. Fortunately, being confined to a wheelchair did not keep him from attending church, regularly. Gwen started to pray for Roger Kelp and thanked God for being merciful toward him.

Her eyelids started to get heavy until a story came on that caught her attention. The World of Religions Day usually referred to as The W.O.R.D., would be in Chicago in June. Gwen had always wanted to attend this event, but it had never come to Louisville, Kentucky. Even if it had, she would not have been able to afford a ticket. With Junior's medical bills and her missing so much time at work, they were struggling to meet their monthly responsibilities. Actually, they were behind on their bills.

Unlike her husband, Gwen's faith was stronger than ever. She did not blame her son's sickness on God, and she continued to pray for a miracle. As strong as her faith was, she sometimes wondered what other religions based their beliefs on. She had researched a few, but she would rather attend a live discussion and hear them express their beliefs in person. This was an event in which at least a hundred different religions of the world gathered in one place, but only the top ten were allowed to speak at the convention. The top holy men of the top ten religions would try to convince the audience that their god was the true God by attempting to debunk and discredit the other religions. She also wondered why a woman was never the top holy person in any of the religions.

Gwen had heard that many people had embraced some of these religions after attending this event. That was one thing in which she was not concerned. She had no problem telling anyone that she had a personal relationship with Jesus and that nothing and nobody could separate the two of them. However, from what she had seen on the news over the years, there always seemed to be as much action outside the event as there was inside. People who objected to one or two of the religions, or all of them, always showed up. The atheists were always present, telling people in all the religions how crazy their beliefs were. Different religious groups argued with each other and carried signs either promoting their religion or ridiculing someone else's.

The W.O.R.D. started as a peaceful event, with its main purpose being to educate people about the different religions of the world; however, over the years it had grown into a recruiting competition with the main strategy being to discredit the competition. No matter where the event was held, it drew the top media coverage from all over the world for the entire weekend.

Gwen closed her eyes and whispered a quick prayer. She prayed that before she was called home to glory that she would be able to attend The W.O.R.D. event at least once. After keeping her eyes closed for a few seconds, she quickly opened them. She pressed her hand a little more firmly on Junior's chest. She moved her hand to different spots on his chest, checking for a heartbeat. She felt his left wrist, searching for a pulse.

"Junior, Junior," she repeated while gently rubbing his chest.

She laid him on the couch and immediately started to administer CPR. She was careful not to press too hard on his small chest while administering the chest compressions. She kept this up for over ten minutes before she saw him take a deep breath. John had just walked into the house. As he entered the house, he froze right in the doorway when he saw his wife trying to resuscitate his son. Gwen was focused on Junior and did not hear John come in the door. When she felt the cool night air hit her back, she turned to see her husband standing in the doorway. Gwen picked up their barely conscious child and handed him to his father.

"Strap him in his car seat while I go get Rose," she commanded as she placed his blanket over the top of him. "We have to take him to the hospital."

John did exactly as his wife had instructed. The initial shock had worn off, and he moved quickly. He was still very concerned about his son, but he was functional. Gwen came out the front door with their daughter in her arms. Rose was still in her pajamas and had a blanket covering her. John ran inside the house, grabbed his keys, locked the door of the house, and ran back to the car. As he slid behind the wheel, he noticed that Gwen had buckled Rose in the front seat next to him, while she had gotten in the back seat with Junior.

"Mommy is Junior ok?" asked Rose.

"He will be, baby; he will be."

John stepped on the gas and sped off while blindly buckling his seatbelt. He hit the emergency flashers as he sped down the street. Gwen kept her hand on Junior's chest to make sure his heart was still beating. She was not sure how long it had stopped before she noticed it. She closed her eyes and lowered her head. At that moment, John looked in the back of the car through the rearview mirror. He saw his wife praying. Gwen's prayer was so focused and so intense that she broke out in a sweat on a cool autumn night. She prayed silently and continuously.

John had seen enough and thought he had better keep his eyes on the road. He was almost certain that his wife was wasting her time. He held out a little bit of hope that the God of Abraham was real, but he didn't feel it. He couldn't talk about his wavering faith with his wife anymore because it always started an argument. Gwen didn't want to listen to anything that might cause her to doubt her faith, especially from someone she loved and respected. He, on the other hand, was tired of praying to a God that never answered his prayers, so he stopped praying. Every so often John would witness something or hear about something that made him think that just maybe God was real, but that feeling never lasted very long. He wanted to believe, but he couldn't recall a single thing in his life that God had helped him with.

With his child's life at stake, he thought he would try God one more time. This was his son, his only son, and he would do anything to save his life. He said a silent prayer. He begged God to save his son. He promised to do anything if God would grant this one request. Tears filled his eyes, and he had to wipe them away so that he could see where he was going. At the end of his prayer, John mouthed the words, "please, God, please."

Suddenly, Gwen opened her eyes and started to move her hand around Junior's chest. His heart had stopped again. She quickly removed him from his safety seat and laid him across the back seat. She knelt down on the floor of the car and started performing CPR all over again.

"In the name of God, John, please hurry," pleaded Gwen as she started the chest compressions.

John pressed the gas pedal to the floor and held on to the steering wheel with everything he had. They were not far from the children's hospital, but every second seemed to drag by. Rose looked through the space between the bucket seats and watched her mother work furiously on her little brother. She knew that what her mother was doing was supposed to help, but it didn't look as if it was working. Tears rolled down both of her cheeks.

"Wake up, Junior! Please wake up. Hurry, Daddy, hurry!" shouted Rose.

They were almost there. John had to stomp on the brake pedal to make the turn toward the emergency room. The hard, right turn rocked Rose from side to side, but her seatbelt kept her from being hurt. Gwen braced herself and held on to Junior, as the car sped toward the emergency room entrance. The tires on the old Chevy squealed as it slid to a stop. John quickly put the car in park, turned off the engine, and took Junior from the arms of his wife all in a matter of seconds. He ran into the hospital with his son. Gwen helped Rose out of her seatbelt, picked her up, and followed her husband inside.

"Somebody help us!" shouted John as the automatic doors opened. "My son can't breathe! Get Dr. Wilkins!"

Gwen and Rose caught up with John at about the same time that two nurses and an emergency room doctor arrived. The emergency room had been slow that night, and there was plenty of staff available to help.

"Call Dr. Wilkins" repeated John. "He's Junior's doctor."

"We need to stabilize him first," explained the emergency room doctor as he took Junior from John's arms and ran into a curtained area. The doctor gently placed the child on a bed and started barking orders to the nurses as he began performing CPR. The nurses ran in two different directions, per the doctor's instructions. One of them closed the curtain and asked the family to have a seat in the waiting area before she left. Gwen handed Rose to John and then walked over to the registration counter. John took a seat and held Rose on his lap.

"I think you need some information from us," said Gwen to the registration nurse.

"Yes, I do, but I was going to give you a few minutes to collect yourselves before I said anything. I saw you rush the child in, and I heard the gentleman over there, who I assume is your husband, ask for Dr. Wilkins. I figured that you are already in our system."

"Yes, that is my husband, and we have been here several times. Our son should be in your files. Dr. Wilkins has been treating him for amyloidosis."

The registration nurse was usually good at controlling her body language, but Gwen still noticed the concern on her face. She knew instantly that the nurse was familiar with her son's condition. Amyloidosis was a rare blood disease that was often classified as a blood cancer. It was frequently referred to as just Amy. It attacked the organs of the body, usually the heart and lungs first, making it difficult for the sufferer to breathe. It was evident that the nurse knew that there was no known cure for this terrible disease.

"I am sorry to hear that," said the nurse, "but he is in good hands. I am sure he will be up and running in no time. Will you complete these forms and bring them back to me when you're finished, please?"

Gwen took the clipboard and pen from the nurse's hand. The truth was she had never seen her son run. He had been sick all his short life, and he hadn't even become skilled at walking yet. Gwen walked over to the waiting area and sat next to her husband. As she started completing the forms, she concentrated on staying focused. She kept her composure as she wrote down her son's name, age, and birthdate. However, she struggled emotionally when she had to list Junior's medications and medical history. She had finished the paperwork and was about to take the clipboard back to the nurse when she heard her daughter sniffling. She turned to Rose and saw tears streaming down her face.

"Don't worry, baby, Junior will be alright," said Gwen as she rubbed her daughter's legs.

"Something is wrong, Mommy," cried Rose. "I can't feel him anymore. He's not here. He's gone," she said as she started to cry harder.

"Calm down, honey," said John. "You're scaring your mother. Don't talk like that. Junior is right over there behind that curtain. He hasn't gone anywhere."

Gwen glanced back and forth between her husband and her daughter. She knew exactly what Rose meant, and she felt that her husband did too. John didn't want to believe it. She had read about close ties between siblings and how they can feel each other's pain or sense when the other is in danger, but that mainly happened between twins. Her husband continued to try to calm Rose down, but she was inconsolable. Somehow Gwen knew that Rose was right and that Junior was gone. As hard as she tried, she could not keep her own eyes from watering.

John realized that he could not calm down Rose, so he looked to his wife for help. He saw tears flowing down her face too. He was frustrated and didn't know what to do. Gwen reached over, grabbed Rose, and placed her on her lap. They clung to each other and just cried.

"Gwen, why are you crying? I was looking to you to help me console Rose. See Rose, I told you that you would upset your mother. The doctor hasn't even told us anything. Why are you two crying like Junior..."

John stopped in mid-sentence as the doctor came from behind the curtain and walked slowly toward them with his head down. Behind the doctor, a nurse dashed from the curtained area with a hand over her mouth. She quickly ran out of sight. The doctor stopped directly in front of them. His eyes were red as if he had been crying. He made a few hand gestures but struggled to find the words.

"I'm sorry; I'm so sorry," he repeated.

John looked up at the doctor, but he was at a loss for words also. He glanced at his wife and daughter, who were still crying in each other's arms. He was starting to feel the pain that they were feeling. He looked around the room and caught the eyes of the registration nurse. She hung her head. Gwen reached out and grabbed his arm, but he pulled away. John got up and slowly walked toward the exit. When he was almost there, he turned around and walked back over to his wife and daughter. He took his car keys from his pocket and put them in his wife's hand.

"You and Rose take the car. I need to walk for a while."

John turned and walked to the exit and left the hospital. He pulled the collar of his jacket up, put his hands in his pockets, and started walking. For the first time since he was a child, John allowed tears to roll down his cheeks. He was numb. He didn't know what to think. He didn't know what direction he was walking in. He wasn't sure how he should feel, but he felt empty, alone, and unimportant. Then his sorrow and emptiness turned to anger. He wiped the tears from his face and placed his hands back in his pockets. He clutched his fists very tightly and mumbled to himself, "There is no God!"

At that moment, a car sped right past him, out of control, and hit a light post. It missed John by a foot at most; he never saw it coming. It came so close to him that it forced him to stop in his tracks. He looked at the smoking, banged-up vehicle and kept walking.

"They're not that far from the hospital," said John. "They will be okay." He kept walking.

"Why should I try to help anyone? No one helped me."

John took a few more steps and then stopped. He turned around and went back to the site of the accident. The driver's side of the car was banged up pretty good, and the driver had to be in bad shape. When he reached the vehicle, the windshield and driver's window were shattered. The male driver was unconscious with blood all over him. He tried to pull the door open but couldn't. At that moment he heard a child crying. He looked in the back seat and saw a young boy strapped in a car seat. He opened the back door and saw that the child's car seat had protected him from serious harm, but the boy was scared. He noticed a trickle of blood on the toddler's forehead, above his left eye near his hairline. He thought it strange that the child had green eyes. He had never seen a male with green eyes, at least not in person. He had seen plenty of females with green eyes but never a guy. John took his handkerchief from his pocket and pressed it against the cut. He talked to the child for a few minutes to calm him down, and the child responded positively to him. He put the child's left hand on the handkerchief and told him to hold it there, and the child did as he was instructed. John shut the door and told the child that he would be back. He was going to get help. He removed the cross from his neck and placed it in the child's right hand. That seemed to pacify the child as he looked it over.

"Here you go, green eyes; you might as well keep this. I don't need it," said John. He walked on, never to return. About a block up the street, John entered a restaurant and made a phone call. He called the hospital and informed them of the accident. He then left the restaurant and walked off into the night.

From across the street, Simon stood in the shadows of a building. He watched John disappear into the darkness. He wanted to console John but now was not the time. For now, he would only observe.

The first year after Junior's death was very hard for Rose. She had bad dreams that caused her to wake up screaming and crying in the middle of the night. She had become withdrawn and depressed and would just start crying sometimes without a warning. Rose started going through a period in which death was always on her mind. She frequently asked her parents if she was going to die. She had gone into a deep, downward spiral and needed professional help. Though money was extremely tight, John and Gwen started taking Rose to see a child psychologist. Her therapy sessions put them in a lot of debt, but the sessions were helpful.

It was months before Rose started to show significant signs of improvement, and she had been in therapy for a little over a year. John and Rose both worked part-time jobs to help pay for her therapy. After ten months of both of them working full-time and part-time jobs, they both received raises within about a month of each other. Gwen was promoted to an Assistant Manager position, and John received a nice raise after his team reached the semifinals of the state tournament.

The raises were not enough to allow them to both quit their part-time jobs right away, but John insisted that they would be ok and convinced Gwen to quit hers. Six months after Rose's last therapy session, John gave up his part-time job. Working around the clock like they were doing kept them busy, and the additional work was therapy for them. Their pain subsided considerably during their busy moments, but it returned on the weekends and during their quiet time. Overcoming their grief paralleled Rose's healing. The better she got, the better they became. They still had rough moments, but they started to subside considerably after two years.

Gwen was determined to stay strong for her daughter. She did not want Rose to see her cry anymore unless they were tears of joy. She struggled almost as much as Rose, but she was better at hiding it and picking her moments. Hiding her emotions from Rose meant that John did not see her as vulnerable as she really was. She came close to a nervous breakdown, and John never had a clue. She cried in the shower and at night after Rose fell asleep. She constantly prayed, asking God for strength and for understanding while tears flowed down her face. She prayed and cried in bed all the time and when she drove back and forth to work. She had occasional weak moments in the presence of Rose, but she would always turn her back, wipe away her tears, and try the best she could to sound cheerful. It always worked, and neither Rose nor John was the wiser.

After months and months of praying, Gwen received the answer she was searching for. God spoke to her while she was cleaning an office before she quit her part-time job. She was cleaning and praying and crying and then Proverbs 3 popped into her head, verses five and six, specifically. God was telling her not to try to understand, just trust in Him and He would direct her path. Gwen knew the verses well. She repeated them to herself over and over again. The more she repeated them, the better she felt. She wiped the tears from her face and finished her cleaning for the night. On her way home, she felt better than she had in a long time. There was still some sadness and grief but no overbearing pain. She felt a sense of relief as if closure had been brought to her pain. She was a God-fearing woman, and she knew that it was time for her to start displaying her faith by trusting God to make everything alright. She knew Junior was not coming back, but she had to believe that her family would be ok. Her walk of faith regarding this particular situation was not easy, but it was necessary because it stabilized her mentally.

As tough as Junior's death was on Gwen and Rose, it was twice as hard for John to cope with the death of his namesake. All three of them needed professional help, but they could only afford to help Rose. John stayed angry all the time and kept to himself a lot. His anger stayed internalized most of the time because he blamed God for allowing Junior to die. He needed an outlet for his anger, and most of the time that outlet was his players. For a while, he was never satisfied with their performance, and he often worked them too hard. His assistant coaches knew he was still hurting, and they intervened on behalf of the guys. He always agreed with his assistants, apologized, and usually asked them to finish the practice without him.

His players knew he was still hurting also, and they never got upset with him. They actually worked harder for him, until their bodies physically gave out. John felt bad during one practice when half of his team started cramping so badly that they needed medical attention. They were all dehydrated. The players still didn't complain, and that shocked John back to reality. He apologized to his players and promised never to push them like that again. He gave them a few days off to rest from the physical part of the practice, and he reminded them that this didn't mean that they didn't have to work hard. The next couple of days they studied their playbook, did some walk throughs on the court and watched game film. After that incident, his personal feelings never affected his work again.

John found another outlet. He increased the frequency of his walks. He took long walks almost every night, sometimes to the point of exhaustion. The pace and distance of his walks depended on the level of his anger. Every time his pace and distance increased, he found himself questioning Christ about his son's death. Jesus attempted to talk to John on many occasions, but John was too angry and too upset to hear anything but his own voice. A few times during his quiet moments he was able to hear the voice of Jesus. He either ignored it or drowned it out with angry thoughts.

John had pretty much stopped going to Church. He did not want to hear Gwen mention Jesus or faith or Church or the Holy Spirit or anything remotely related to Christianity. Gwen's faith was getting stronger, but John's had gone in the opposite direction, and this had caused more than a few arguments. John never cursed God, but he wasn't praising Him either. Gwen learned to pick her moments. She was determined to never give up and to continue to pray for her family. She knew how deep John's hurt was, and she knew she had to be patient, for as long as it took.

CHAPTER 6

BACK IN THE BLUEGRASS

Louisville, Kentucky – Twenty Years Later

Simon had traveled all over the country in the last twenty years, but he had spent the majority of his time in the Deep South. That was the area in this city in which his people seemed to be in the most distress. He was back in Louisville, Kentucky, but he knew that his work in the Deep South was not finished. Jesus had allowed him to help his people through the civil rights movement before he ever stepped foot in Kentucky, and there was much more work to do.

Jesus had commanded Simon to return to Kentucky to finish his assignment there. Though John and Gwendolyn Crenshaw lived in an area of town known as Newburg, Simon was currently walking the streets in the western end of the city. This was the area of the city in which most of the African Americans lived, and he always wanted to know how his people were doing. Simon wore modern clothes to blend in with everyone else, but he always wore sandals, regardless of the weather. The blood of Jesus still glowed brightly on his hands and wrists and protected him from everything, even severe weather. He was enjoying the cool breeze on his face on this warm summer night.

His people were still struggling in Louisville, but that was all part of the civil rights movement that he had watched so closely in the south. The movement had swept the whole country like a tidal wave, but some parts of the country benefited more than others. The civil rights movement was over fifty years old, but improvement had been slow. Problems were not being resolved; they were being camouflaged. The movement had hit Kentucky decades ago, but it was not strong in the state. Kentucky did not have enough vocal leaders. However, this was the problem in most states. There was plenty of work but few laborers.

As Simon walked up Riverpark, headed to downtown Louisville, he contemplated the biggest difference between people today and those in his time. Today's individuals were too self-centered to be passionate about anything, but themselves. If they did not personally benefit in some way, they were not interested in taking a stand. In his day, no one had much of anything, but what they had they shared. Back then, man had more of a sense of community. They were especially passionate about their religion, whatever it was, even if they did not believe in the God of Abraham. Now, not only are the nonbelievers more passionate in their nonbelief, but the so-called believers act as if the word of God is an inconvenience to them.

Simon understood his mission very well. The work was often tough, but he was still grateful that Jesus had chosen him. The more wealth people accumulated, the less they needed God. People today were never satisfied. They want more and more possessions, and technology had made it easier to work, communicate, and play. Why should people pray when technology had become their god? They could create their own miracles and then sit back and marvel at their genius.

When individuals take the time to pray today, their prayers are all about what they need or occasionally about a loved one or friend. In his day, if a man could help his neighbor, he did so without hesitation. Now, everyone was trying to hold on to what they had. Simon saw that his work was abundant. Not only did he have to keep that remnant of true and active believers encouraged and hopeful, but he had to help those distracted believers to get back to the Word, to remember God's promises, to walk by faith, and to get busy spreading the good news and helping others.

Then there were the nonbelievers and the confused. The nonbelievers were like the apostle Paul before his Damascus road experience. Sometimes they had to be knocked down and blinded before Jesus could get their attention. However, once they were in a situation in which all their knowledge, science, and technology were useless, they usually came around to Jesus. The confused were similar to the nonbelievers in that they usually had exhausted all other possibilities until God was the only answer. However, the confused were usually active believers once who had suffered a great loss. Their loss turned them away from God. Way deep down inside they still believed, but they suppressed it so much that they began to relate more to the world than to Christ. They needed more than a miracle. They needed to personally experience Christ. John S. Crenshaw fell in the confused category.

Simon's thoughts were interrupted by an intense sensation. He could feel a lot of energy in the air, and he decided to follow it until he found its source. In doing so, he crossed over to the seventh block of Jefferson Street. A block up the street was half a dozen police cars surrounding a midsize, four-door vehicle right at the corner of Sixth and Jefferson. The red and blue lights on the police cars were flashing, and he could see officers pointing their weapons at the surrounded vehicle. A Black man emerged from the vehicle with his hands held high over his head. Simon walked within a hundred feet of the scene, but the officers hadn't noticed him.

The suspect turned, faced the opposite direction, and dropped his hands behind his back as he was instructed to do. As one of the officers walked up to him and began placing handcuffs on his wrists, the other officers holstered their weapons. Rodney was going through some hard times, and being caught stealing a car wasn't going to make things better. He had never been in trouble with the law before, but his kids were hungry. His small business was experiencing difficult times, and he had no other source of income. He had had no intention of committing a crime. He decided to take a walk to clear his head and to think. He thought about closing his business and getting a regular job. He had put in dozens of applications, but no one had called and his wife was between jobs. He saw a car idling in front of a small store, and no one was in it. Though he was not a criminal, he knew of a few seedy characters who would give him good money for the car. Less than a mile down the road, he regretted what he had done. He had driven around for a while trying to decide what to do. He had decided to abandon the car, and his idea to make a quick profit when he was pulled over. As he was being cuffed, Rodney looked up and saw Simon. He stared at the man with the noticeably red hands. His attention was so fixed on Simon that he did not hear the officer instruct him to get into his cruiser. The officer waited on Rodney as he held open the door of the cruiser.

"You're not going to like it if I have to help you get into this car," said the officer.

The officer wondered what had so thoroughly caught Rodney's attention. He looked over in Simon's direction, as did the other officers. They saw a tall, muscular Black man who had blood all over his hands. As the officers gathered together, they instinctively placed their hands on their weapons.

"And we thought this was going to be a boring night," said Lt. Perkins, who was the highest-ranked officer on the scene.

By now a few bystanders had gathered across the street. They talked among themselves and watched with intense interest. The officers spread out, forming a half-circle as they slowly approached Simon. They wanted to cover as much area as they could in case he decided to run.

"Hey you, with the bloody hands, stay where you are. We want to talk to you," said the Lieutenant. "Keep your hands where we can see them, and don't try to run."

"I think you want more from me than conversation, and why would I run?" asked Simon.

"What is your name and why are your hands so bloody?" asked the Lieutenant, as he firmly grasped his weapon and removed the safety.

"You will not believe me if I tell you," said Simon.

"Probably not," said the Lieutenant, "but it's a starting point."

"My name is Simon, and I wear the blood of Jesus on my hands. Why are you ready to use your weapon on me? I am not a threat to you, and I have done nothing wrong."

"I'll ask the questions. We will use our weapons only if you force us to."

"You do not believe me, so where do we go from here?" asked Simon.

Simon was now completely surrounded by the other officers. Two of the officers had their pistols drawn and pointed at him. The bystanders across the street had pulled out their phones and had started to record the incident with their cameras. No one had noticed that the car thief had slipped off into the night.

"This is not going to end pretty if you don't cooperate and tell me the truth."

"Are you anxious to harm me?" Simon asked.

"I don't want to harm anyone. I just want to know why you're walking down the street in the middle of the night looking as if you just murdered someone."

"I would like to know what crime I have committed, and why two of your men have their weapons pointed at my back?"

"I am trying to figure out what crime you have committed. Their weapons are drawn because your hands are bloody, and you do not have a good explanation. We're obligated to question you based on reasonable suspicion. Why would anyone believe that the blood on your hands is from someone who died over two thousand years ago?"

"I can understand why you do not believe me, but Jesus is alive."

"Ok, I'm tired of talking. This is going nowhere. Put your hands behind your back; you're under arrest. We will probably have to run you by the hospital first to find out what drugs you're on."

Simon stood his ground and did not move as the officers inched closer to him. The Lieutenant removed his cuffs from his belt. The two officers who had their pistols drawn holstered them and pulled out Tasers.

"Turn around and put your hands behind your back. I am not going to tell you again," said the Lieutenant.

"I will not be shackled," said Simon.

"We can do this the easy way or the hard way. I prefer the easy way, but my guys would love to pump a hundred thousand volts of electricity into you."

"Darkness," said Simon.

Instantly, there was total darkness within a two-mile radius. The streetlights were no longer shining, no cellphones were lit up, and even the lights on the police cruisers, which were flashing just moments earlier, were dark. You could not even see the stars in the sky. There was a complete absence of light. Though there was not much traffic on the streets, tires could be heard screeching a couple of blocks over. Drivers were hitting their brakes trying to avoid hitting what they could not see. The police and the bystanders started to mumble. They could not see their hands in front of their face, and they were scared. One officer fired his Taser, and the other followed suit. They heard the thud of the darts striking its target and then heard a body hit the ground. They smiled about the accuracy of their shots. One of the officers pulled a small flashlight from his pocket, but it would not work. They soon learned that Simon was gone, and it was their Lieutenant whom they had tasered.

The lights came back on after what seemed like an eternity. In actuality, it had been only about a minute. Simon was nowhere to be seen, and the Lieutenant was still shaking from receiving fifty bolts of electricity. He was lucky that one of the officers had missed him. As they helped their commander back to his car, they noticed that the car thief had gotten away, too. They knew that as soon as the Lieutenant regained his strength, they would receive an ear full.

"I'll deal with you idiots later," said the Lieutenant, "but for now call for backup. We have to find that guy before he hurts someone else."

"But sir," said one of the officers, "didn't you see what he just did? He said one word; he said 'darkness,' and it became completely dark out here. I couldn't see anything. Even the lights on our cruisers stopped flashing, which, by the way, are now flashing again."

"It was just some sort of power failure," said the Lieutenant, "a blackout. Cities have blackouts all the time. It's just fortunate for him that it happened when it did."

"Sir, a blackout would not cause the lights on our cruiser to go out. My flashlight wouldn't come on, but now it's working again," said the officer as he clicked his flashlight off and on.

"Sargent, I don't have time to discuss Einstein's Theory of Relativity with you. Call for backup as I ordered and let's go find this guy."

"Yes, sir!"

The officers jumped in their cruisers and sped off in different directions, looking for Simon. Within moments a half dozen more cruisers had joined the search. A bike patrol searched the alleys and side streets. Little did they know that Simon was on the other end of town, walking through some of the neighborhoods of Newburg.

Gwen had just finished her shower and was about to sit down to watch the late news as she always did. First, she wanted to check on Trey, her grandson. She walked into his room and tiptoed over to his bed. He was fast asleep. Gwen and John watched their grandson often to give their daughter and her husband a break. Things were going well for the young couple. They were living with Gwen and John to save money for their own place. Tony played ball for John in high school, and that's how he met Rose. Gwen and John both liked Tony and agreed that he was very mature for his age.

Gwen and John were exhausted. Trey was a ball of energy. He was the typical two-year-old in almost every aspect, except one. He tired easily. He suffered from the same disease that claimed the life of his uncle, but he was a much stronger child. He had his bad days, but they were not as frequent or as debilitating as Junior's episodes were. Trey was named in honor of his grandfather and his uncle. Since Rose's married name was Thompson, her son couldn't be John Samuel Crenshaw III, so she named him Trey Nathaniel. Rose and her husband, along with her parents, liked the idea that Trey's initials were TNT. Junior was three years old when he passed away, and John had taken it extremely hard. He tried to distance himself from Trey when they learned that he had the same rare blood disease as Junior. All he could think about was one day losing Trey as he had lost Junior, and he did not want to ride that emotional roller coaster ever again. He tried to harden his heart and withhold his love. However, that became more difficult as the months passed. Trey was never as sickly as Junior, and he followed John around the house wherever he went. Before he could walk, Trey would always crawl to his grandpa.

John's attempts to escape from Trey evolved into games of hide-and-seek, which led to silly discussions, which eventually developed into games of catch. Gwen knew that John was devastated when Junior died and that he did not want to experience that hurt ever again. However, she never tried to convince him to hold or play with his grandson. She believed that only an evil, hateful, possessed person could completely distance themselves from their grandchild, and John was no such person. Gwen knew that time was on her side, but there were some difficult days.

When they found out that Rose was having a child, John threatened to kick Rose out of the house. He was never thrilled with the news of her pregnancy because she didn't get married until she became pregnant. However, he had already lost a son, and he didn't want to be estranged from his daughter. Waiting on the birth of their grandchild was hard on John. He started to relive the death of Junior, and he started to hurt all over again. He stayed withdrawn for a long time. Trey was about three months old before John showed signs of improvement.

The fact that Trey never looked sickly helped tremendously. John was able to enjoy Trey more before he even realized how fond he had become of him. He was never able to laugh and play with Junior as he was able to do with Trey. He never felt Junior pull on his pant leg or experience him reaching out his arms to him.

Gwen thought about all this as she checked the baby monitor and camera. She knew they were working perfectly, but it was a habit that she couldn't break. Though Trey appeared perfectly healthy, she could not forget that he was sick. She walked back into the living room once she was satisfied that her grandson was okay. She returned just in time to see the beginning of the late news. John was taking a shower. The first story covered The W.O.R.D. convention that was coming to Louisville. Gwen had already heard about this and had purchased two tickets a year ago when the venue first made them available to the public. No matter what the cost, she was not going to miss it this year. They were coming to her hometown, and she would never have a better opportunity to see it. She bought a ticket for John, hoping that he would go with her. He had told her that he wasn't interested, but he never said that he would not go. Even if he didn't go, Gwen had a few friends in mind who she knew she could count on if John decided not to go. Her best friend, Frances, had already put in her bid for the ticket.

After the commercial break, a breaking story came on that caught Gwen's attention. It showed a Black man with bloody hands surrounded by police officers. Simon's encounter with the police was playing out right before her eyes. One of the bystanders had sent his recording to the television station. The story began with the police walking over to Simon and questioning him.

A chill went through Gwen's body when Simon answered the officer's question about the blood on his hands. The news anchor spun the story as some type of anomaly because of the blackout. To the media, the arrest was no big deal, but a total blackout, including the lights on the police cars, was the story. Gwen couldn't understand why Simon was never mentioned or referred to during the report. She couldn't explain it, but she felt there was something special about him. She was thoroughly convinced that her feelings were correct when she saw the man utter one word, "darkness," and then the screen went black. When she heard the officer explain that even the lights on their police cruisers went dark, Gwen knew this was more than a coincidence and definitely not a blackout.

Little did Gwen know that only a select few could see or hear Simon on the news broadcast. To the rest of the viewers, Simon was never on-screen and could not be heard. They could see and hear the police talking to someone. They even saw the blackout and the return of the light, but they never saw or heard Simon. At the time, Gwen surmised that the total absence of any reference to Simon was racial profiling; just another black man doing something criminal. That was not a big story for the media unless the black man was well known or affluent. Simon would learn of the broadcast later, but at the time even he did not know that Jesus had allowed only a select few to witness and hear him on it.

The station went to a commercial break, and Gwen could not get Simon out of her mind. She ignored the rest of the news and grabbed her Bible. She quickly turned to the New Testament and went to the books of Matthew, Mark, and Luke. She flipped through the pages and read the story of the crucifixion in each book. She knew that the arrest and crucifixion were the only Scriptures in the Bible that talked about Jesus bleeding. Each book identified Simon of Cyrene as the man who helped Jesus carry his cross. The book of Mark went a bit further and identified him as the father of Alexander and Rufus.

He had two sons, pondered Gwen, *he would understand. He would be over two thousand years old*, she thought. *How could that be?* The ringing of the baby monitor startled her. She ran into Trey's room. John had just finished his shower and was putting on his bathrobe when he heard the ringing sound. As he stepped out of the bathroom to investigate, he saw his wife bent over Trey, pressing on his chest. John's heart hit the floor.

CHAPTER 7

PREPARING FOR THE W.O.R.D.

All the hotels in Louisville, Kentucky, were buzzing with activity. Every hotel and motel room within a hundred-mile radius of the city was booked to capacity. Every restaurant had a waiting list of at least forty-five minutes, and traffic was ridiculous. People from every imaginable location were pouring into Louisville to attend The W.O.R.D. event. Revenue was up in the city, but patience was at an all-time low.

With so many different people gathering in one place, skirmishes were frequently breaking out, which was ironic for people coming together to attend a religious event. A heavy presence of law enforcement could be seen in the streets. Officers from the neighboring states of Indiana, Ohio, and Tennessee arrived a week in advance to help. Additional law enforcement, in the form of federal agents, had come to town to join their local counterparts. At least a dozen bomb-sniffing K-9 units were in the city. Every precaution was being taken to protect the city from terrorists and any other type of low-life criminal who had descended on the city within the last five years.

Since its beginning, the W.O.R.D. event had been the biggest event of the year, no matter where it was held. It easily qualified as the largest event in the history of Louisville. The city had been awarded the event five years earlier and had been preparing for it since the announcement was made. Not only had additional law enforcement been brought in, but five hundred additional beds had been secured in jails in the surrounding area. Many people in the law-enforcement community suspected that would probably not be enough.

This was the only event in the world in which all of the world's superpowers shared intelligence and manpower to identify, isolate, and capture the undesirables of the world. The security was so intense, that precautions and vetting took place as soon as a host city was announced. The FBI, CIA, and Homeland Security had a presence in Louisville a week after the city was awarded the event. The KGB, Interpol, and other law enforcement agencies from around the world set up shop in the city a couple of weeks later.

The media coverage was insane. News media from every country in the world, even those territories not recognized as countries, were represented in the city. Every journalist was looking for that original story that no one else had. Every photographer was looking for that perfect shot, from that impossible angle that no one else could get. During the week of the W.O.R.D. event, nothing else in the world seemed to matter, especially in the host city. Some said that the media coverage paralleled what they would imagine for the return of Christ himself.

Since the third year of this event, the federal government had donated at least a billion dollars to the host city, and in some cases, this was not close to being enough money. The money went to building additional hotels; hiring additional law enforcement and first responders; bringing in more interpreters, limousine drivers, and taxi services; and securing a large number of food vendors that only supplied the host city during the week of the event.

Of all the events that took place during the week of the W.O.R.D., the Parade of Faith was second only to the main event itself. Though only the top ten religions of the world were allowed to speak at the event, the Parade of Faith was open to any religion that paid the entry fee. The number-one-ranked religion, according to the number of followers it had, was awarded the privilege of naming the parade. Christianity had held those honors ever since the event started, and the parade had always been named the Parade of Faith. However, the Nation of Islam was quickly gaining ground.

The top religion could also choose their location in the parade. Though the Christians had been number one every year, they always preferred to march from the middle of the parade, and this year was no different. The parade was indeed a spectacle to behold.

The universal Christian church didn't have a single person designated as their religious leader, like the other religions, although many Roman Catholics believed it should be the pope. The sitting Pope had attended every convention of the W.O.R.D., but the representative for the Christians had always been the CEO of the Faith Led Disciples. The Faith Led Disciples was an international Christian organization, much like the Southern Baptist Convention, whose primary focus was the Great Commission. The Faith Led Disciples owned several large transportation companies, which included airlines, cruise ships, bus companies, and even cab services. This allowed them to go anywhere at any time. Although the Faith Led Disciples and the Pope had an international presence, the W.O.R.D. event was started in the United States and had its headquarters in the United States. Its founder was a former Faith Led Disciples' pastor who mandated, through the bylaws, that the Christian representatives of the W.O.R.D. event must always be the top executives of the Faith Led Disciples. He reasoned that, according to the Bible, the antichrist was supposed to come from one of the Macedonian-Greek Empires of Alexander the Great. Therefore, he reasoned that if the head of the Faith Led Disciples was always the Christian representative of the W.O.R.D convention, the antichrist or any other demon would not be able to easily infiltrate the organization and contaminate it. Therefore, the gospel would always be communicated truthfully according to the Bible; hence the acronym they used to name the event.

An estimated one million people lined the parade route. This did not include the people hanging out of windows and perched on rooftops. Fifty floats and more than three hundred participants lined up on Baxter Avenue. This included the various choirs, politicians, celebrities, and dignitaries who had been selected to march in the parade.

The parade route was set to be two miles long, which was an unusually long route for a parade, but all of the W.O.R.D. parades had been long. The city had blocked off several streets, and these closures were announced months in advance. Usually, every street within a mile radius of the parade route was closed two days before the parade. That was mainly for security purposes. The W.O.R.D. event brought in so much revenue for the host city, that the contractual conditions of the event had never been declined by a city it had approached.

One thing was very evident when the parade started. All the groups were very serious about the religion they represented. The representatives waved and bowed to the crowd, but very few smiled. Each religious group had decorated their float with the most recognizable image or symbol of their religion. They displayed holy garments, the Quran, the spiritual third eye of the Hindu, the Tora, the crucifixion cross and the Holy Bible, the statues of Buddha and other India-based religions, among many other religious signs and symbols. The participants stood tall and proud with every step they took.

There was one very curious observer as the parade went up Main Street. Simon tried to blend in with the crowd as he focused on the float of the Christians. The crucifixion rising from an open Bible was the most impressive float; at least that's what Simon thought. There was a real person attached to the cross, who was very convincing. Simon was in awe. This depiction of the crucifixion was a bit flawed, but it was realistic enough to bring back memories of a day he would never forget.

Simon had been hiding his hands in his pockets to keep from drawing attention to himself, as he made his way to the front of the crowd to get a better look. As he stood and gazed at the float, he began to have flashbacks of that dreadful day. Though he now knew that the crucifixion of Christ was predestined, the memory of the terror and distress that he experienced that day stayed with him. He remembered the lightning and the thunder and the hard rain that pummeled him as he curled up in a ball in an attempt to protect himself. Most of all Simon remembered the darkness. After the storm had eased, the darkness lingered on. The pitch-black stillness was the most unnerving thing of all. It was as if the whole world had died, and he was waiting to feel the sting of death.

A slight sting in his back instantly brought Simon back from his trip down memory lane. It was more irritating than painful, and he felt in his spirit that there were evil intentions behind it. As he slowly turned around, he saw four police officers directly behind him, and one of them had just tasered him. He noticed that the crowd of people who were just around him had started to back away, but almost all of them had their cell phones out with their cameras pointed at him. Though all the officers had their Tasers drawn and pointed at him, Lieutenant Perkins was holding the one connected to the dart in his back.

"I had a feeling that the man who claimed to have helped Jesus would be interested in this parade," said the Lieutenant. Just when the Lieutenant was about to say something else, he watched Simon pull the dart from his back. The fifty volts of electricity that had just entered his body had no effect on him. "Hit him again," barked the Lieutenant.

A second officer fired a dart into Simon's chest. Again, Simon pulled the dart out. The other two officers fired simultaneously and hit him in the chest again. Once again, Simon removed the darts from his body. All four officers holstered their Taser and drew their service pistol.

"I don't know how you're still standing after two hundred thousand volts of electricity flowed through your body," said the Lieutenant, "but you are coming with us dead or alive. You choose."

Simon and the Lieutenant stood face-to-face, and Simon started to become angry. He had seen these weapons in action, and he knew what they could do. He was not concerned for himself, but there were a lot of innocent bystanders around. He quickly said a prayer to himself, and Jesus answered him immediately. *Do not act. Submit to these authority figures for now.* Simon relaxed and obeyed the command of Jesus.

"What will you have me do?" asked Simon.

"Now that's the type of attitude that will help you stay alive," said the Lieutenant. "Turn around and put your hands behind your back."

Simon did as he was instructed. He did not resist, but it took every bit of restraint he could muster as the handcuffs were fastened around his wrists. All he could think about was when his people were hunted and shackled like animals. If he didn't change his focus, Simon knew he would not be able to be obedient. He stopped concentrating on his discomfort and started focusing on obeying Jesus.

Simon ignored the long stares and turned-up noses he received as he was being escorted to the patrol car. He continued to marvel at the creative floats as he walked. A sudden sadness came over him, but it was not because of the handcuffs he wore. As he looked at the floats, he thought about all the misguided people who did not know Jesus. The floats represented the beliefs of millions of people, and this did not include the atheists, who were present in the city in record numbers.

Every float, except one, represented a religion other than Christianity. The reason for his obedience had never been clearer than at that moment. For the first time since being in the service of Jesus, Simon realized what was at stake. He understood that his service was much more important than coming to the aid of any one person. Millions of souls were at stake, and he knew that the little success he had experienced thus far paled in comparison to the work that still needed to be done. There were so many misguided and misinformed people who were in danger of eternal damnation. He knew that all of them would not be saved, but he was sure that every one of them was worth the effort. This calmed him as he began to feel overwhelmed.

The police officers approached an alley and instructed Simon to turn into it. He saw two police cruisers parked a few yards away. Both vehicles had their headlights flashing. One of the officers opened the back door of the first car and motioned for Simon to get into that vehicle. The officer helped him to bend down into the car. Simon had been around thousands of cars before but had never ridden in one. This first ride was uncomfortable because his hands were cuffed behind his back and he had very little leg room. Lieutenant Perkins and another officer got into the first vehicle while the other two officers got into the second one.

Both cruisers began to move forward and slowly exited the alley. The red and blue lights on each one began to flash, and the parade attendees made an opening to allow the vehicles to pass through. The police cruisers interrupted the parade as they slowly went up Main Street, forcing the floats and all the marchers to one side of the street or the other. Only a few of the people who witnessed Simon's arrest would remember it once the cruisers were out of sight.

Simon was enjoying the ride, even though it was a relatively short one. He had a close-up view of the parade from the back seat of the cruiser. He could have almost forgotten about his predicament if the handcuffs were not hurting his wrists. He ordered the handcuffs to open, and they obeyed. He set them on the seat beside him as he continued to watch the parade from the patrol car.

After a few minutes, and a few turns, the cruisers came to a stop in front of a correctional facility. All four officers got out of the vehicles and gathered near the driver's side door of the first cruiser. One of the officers opened the passenger door and ordered Simon to get out. As he scooted toward the door, they could see that his hands were free. All four officers drew their service pistols and pointed them at him. Simon got out of the car and made eye contact with Lieutenant Perkins.

"What happened to the cuffs?" asked the Lieutenant.

"They are on the seat of the vehicle," said Simon. "They hurt my wrists, and I don't like being shackled. I will not be a threat to you. I will comply with your demands."

"Hold your hands out in front of you," ordered Perkins.

Simon did as he was instructed, and one of the officers immediately placed a pair of handcuffs on him.

"I don't know how you removed the other pair," said Perkins, "but if you want to stay healthy, don't let it happen again. Follow me."

All the officers holstered their weapons. They surrounded Simon as the Lieutenant led them inside the facility. Before they entered the building, the officer directly behind Simon slumped to the ground.

"Revive him," ordered Jesus.

CHAPTER 8

WHERE IS GOD?

John and Gwen waited for the doctor to bring them good news about Trey. Gwen sat patiently, but John was a bit agitated. He couldn't sit still. He turned from side to side. He folded his arms across his chest one minute and sat on his hands the next. He got up and paced back and forth across the floor, went and looked out of the emergency room door for a few minutes, and then came back and sat down. Gwen did not say anything to him. She knew this was hard on him, as it was her, and his restless energy was his way of coping with this situation.

Rose and Tony hurriedly came through the emergency room doors and rushed straight to Gwen and John. Gwen explained to them what had happened. Trey was in a room down the hall, and the doctor was still examining him.

Rose had tears running down her cheeks, and they all tried to comfort her. As hard as this was on everyone, it was especially hard on Rose. She remembered this feeling from twenty years earlier when she lost her brother; when she knew that he had left her. That horrible feeling haunted her for a couple of years, and now it was back, and she was scared. Tony put his arm around her and pulled her close, trying to comfort her.

Rose took a quick glance over at her mom. Gwen appeared to be holding up well, but Rose knew this was a difficult time for her mother also. She lost her only son, and now she could lose her only grandson.

She always appeared to be the strongest person in the family, and she hardly ever saw her mother cry or get bent out of shape. It was no question that her faith was strong, but Rose felt she held too much inside.

John could not stand to see his little girl cry. Not again, he thought as he got up and paced the floor. Here he was twenty years later in the same hospital, concerned about his grandson, who had the same illness his son had. God did not answer his prayers when his son died, which was the last time he prayed, so why should he pray now. Besides, he had been told a long time ago that you shouldn't call on God only when you need or want something. You're supposed to have a relationship with him. It's hard to have a relationship with him if you never talk to him.

He told himself several times that Jesus was a fairy tale in which the poor and downtrodden clung to because they had no other source of hope. It made them feel good if they were in a bad situation to think that Jesus walked the earth and healed all kinds of people and performed all types of miracles. If he healed them, then he could heal me, was their misguided reasoning. Where was God when Junior needed healing? Where is God now when Trey needs help?

John tried to take his mind off God. It was just upsetting him more. He sat back down beside his wife. Gwen grabbed his hand and held it in hers. Her calmness helped to calm him. Her faith in God was strong and sometimes contagious. John remembered certain times in his life when he thought that maybe Jesus was real and maybe he was alive. He had seen things or felt things or heard others testify about things that sent him into deep thought about what he had just experienced. Then he would think about the rough life he had endured and about all the times he called on Jesus, but Jesus never answered his prayers.

John suddenly remembered a dream he had a couple of years after Junior died. At least he thought it was a dream, but he wasn't sure. He was watching television late one night when he heard a voice call his name. At first, he thought that it was Gwen, but she had already gone to bed, and it sounded like a man's voice. Again, and again the voice called out to him, but John ignored it because he thought he was dreaming. Then he received the shock of his life. The voice asked him why he was ignoring the Son of man. *"When will you talk to me,"* the voice asked. John stood up and looked around the room. No one was there but him.

John responded, "The son of man is not real." "Even if he is, why would I talk to him? He didn't want to talk to me when I needed him." John picked up the remote and turned the television off. "I must have been dreaming," he said. He got up from his chair and went to bed.

That dream came to him every once in a while, and he wasn't sure why he was thinking about it now. He didn't realize that Jesus called out to him whenever he started to think for just a moment that maybe Jesus was real, and maybe praying would make a difference. Those few moments of belief were an invitation for Jesus to enter his life. Jesus had always heard John's prayers and had reached out to him on many occasions. However, John never exercised his faith, so doubt and fear always drowned out the voice of Jesus.

Regardless of the hurt, he was feeling, John could not get that dream out of his head. Why would Christ call out to him, someone who had ignored God all his life? Why would Jesus want to talk to him now? John turned his head away from his wife and wiped a tear from his eye. He didn't know what to do or think. He just knew that he wanted Trey to grow up and live a normal, healthy, long life. If God were real, where is He?

Gwen was sure that she heard a muffled sniffle come from her husband, but she knew better than to bring it up, even in an attempt to encourage him. She never said a word about it and didn't turn in his direction. She just squeezed his hand a little tighter. She was concerned that John would die a spiritual death, and maybe even a physical one if anything happened to Trey. She still had hope that her husband would eventually invite and accept Jesus into his life. She saw signs of his faith every so often, even though he tried to hide it. She couldn't say anything to him about Jesus because it would start an argument. He would bring up all the times in his life when he needed Jesus but was let down. It would just reopen old wounds. She prayed on it every day and decided to put it in the Lord's hands. She knew that Satan was trying to keep her husband down. Even now the enemy was at work placing that little seed of doubt in her mind. She was concerned for John because of what might happen to Trey. Of course, she was concerned about Tony and Rose too, but Tony appeared to be holding up pretty well. He was being strong for Rose. Gwen said a quick prayer and refused to believe that it would not be answered to her satisfaction.

John started to get a little fidgety again. They had been there a couple of hours now and had not heard anything about Trey's condition. He got up and paced the floor again. At that moment, a few of John's players came through the emergency room door. Tony had kept in touch with some of them and had called them and informed them of Trey's situation. They all wanted to support their coach.

"Hey Coach, how are things going?" asked one of the players.

"Hey Rev, what are you guys doing here?"

"We're a team, Coach. What happens to one of us, happens to all of us."

Rev was the captain of the team and the most talented player. He was a senior, and he and a couple of his teammates had heard from several division-one colleges. His real name was Ezekiel Jackson, but his friends called him Rev, which was short for Revelations. His teammates had given him that name. He loved to respond to trash-talking opponents by telling them that they needed to go to church, and he was just the person to take them. And just like the last book of the Bible, Rev foretold what was about to happen and that there was nothing they could do to stop him. This usually happened during some type of scoring play in which he always made good on his promise. A couple of his teammates call him a prophet, but he liked Rev better. He had never heard of anyone else having that nickname. Ezekiel was from a single-parent home, and his mother named him after her father. Ezekiel's mother idolized her father, who was named after the Old Testament prophet.

John didn't realize it, but his team was just what he needed. He always talked to them about persevering through tough situations, not just tough games. None of his players had ever seen him throw a pity party, and he subconsciously went into mentor mode as soon as he saw them. His attitude and posture improved as he greeted them. John was well thought of and nationally known at this point in his career. He had turned down numerous college coaching offers, and it was not unusual to see college scouts at their games. He had won seven state championships in the last fifteen years and had at least one player to receive a scholarship from a division-one college every year for the last ten years. A couple of his former players had been first-round NBA draft choices, and another dozen or so were drafted in later rounds. He wasn't in it for the money. He liked transforming boys into mature, responsible young men. He had never had a player fail to graduate from high school. Seventy-five percent of his players attended college on either an athletic or an academic scholarship. The other twenty-five percent went into either the service or a trade school.

The parents loved him and came from all over the country to have their sons play for him. They knew that he would bring out the best in their kids. The college coaches loved him because they knew that his players had a high basketball IQ, went to class, and never had behavioral issues.

Gwen knew that John's team was what he needed right now, and he was truly glad to see them. This was a good time for her to check on Trey since John was with his team and Tony was comforting Rose. She got up and slowly walked over to the receptionist's desk to inquire about her grandson. The receptionist was very friendly, and she excelled at comforting and encouraging the family of the patients. She always knew the right thing to say, and she was also so sincere. Gwen loved talking to Liz. She had met her before when she brought Trey in a few times for checkups.

"How are you doing, Mrs. Crenshaw?" asked Liz as Gwen approached the desk.

"I'm doing fine," said Gwen. "How many times do I have to tell you to call me Gwen? How is my grandson doing?"

"He must be doing well. No news is good news. You know that you would be the first to know if I heard anything about that darling grandson of yours. I'm pretty sure you will be hearing something soon."

"Thanks, Liz, you always make me feel better."

"Thank you, Mrs. ...uh..., thank you, Gwen. Dr. Richards will be here soon. Have you ever met him?"

"I don't think so. Who is Dr. Richards?"

"He's the intern whose blood has been used for years in the research for the cure to amyloidosis. I heard that there has been a lot of success recently."

"Oh Lord, I almost forgot about him. Please don't say anything about this to my husband. I haven't told him that I gave samples of Junior's blood to use in their research with Dr. Richards' blood. I was hoping that some good would come out of Junior's death."

"I understand," said Liz. "I won't say anything to him, but I think you should tell him."

"You're right, and I will. I should have told him long ago, but I don't think this is a good time."

"Gwen, this is not bad news. Why do you think this will be a difficult conversation? I think your husband would be glad to know that his son's blood was helping to find a cure for the disease that took his life."

"You're probably right, Liz. It's just hard to have any kind of conversation about Junior. John took it so hard when he died that we rarely talk about him. That's why I'm so concerned about him now. He has gotten so close to Trey. I don't know if he can survive if something happens to him. Is progress really being made on a cure for that dreadful disease?"

"That's what I hear," said Liz. "It seems that significant progress has been made with the samples taken from your son. The doctors have been actively seeking amyloidosis patients to test the serum made from the mixture of Dr. Richards' blood and your son's blood."

"Why is it taking so long? Junior passed away twenty years ago. Will Trey benefit from the progress that has been made?"

"I don't know. It's a possibility. Here comes Dr. Richards now. I'll introduce you two."

"No, not now Liz. John might overhear us."

Gwen went and sat back down beside Rose and Tony. She watched Dr. Richards as he stopped to chat with Liz. Though he was still an intern, Dr. Richards was highly respected around the hospital. Gwen remembered reading an article about him six months ago. It talked about how mature he was for his age and how dedicated and bright he was. Though his blood was being used in amyloidosis research, he was studying to become a heart surgeon. Gwen remembered reading that his father had died of a massive heart attack while they were on their way to pick up his mother from the hospital, which was the same night that Junior had died.

When Dr. Richards took a quick glance back at her, she felt a little embarrassed. She knew that Liz had said something to him about her. She looked away and concentrated on her daughter. Rose had calmed down, and Gwen thanked God for Tony. John was still talking to his players, and she suddenly felt all alone. Dr. Richards had finished his conversation with Liz and was walking down the hall. Gwen's eyes followed him until he was out of sight. Before she looked away, she noticed that Dr. Rosen was coming toward them. Dr. Rosen was Trey's doctor.

It appeared that everyone had noticed Dr. Rosen heading their way. Tony, Rose, John, and Gwen all walked toward him simultaneously. The ball players started to follow, but Ezekiel convinced them to stay behind. He reminded them that this was a family moment and that they could wait a few minutes longer to find out what was going on with the coach's grandson. They waited in the lobby area and observed the facial expressions and body language of everyone. The family and the doctor discussed Trey's situation near the hallway entrance.

"What's going on doctor?" asked Rose. "How is Trey doing?"

"Our son is okay, isn't he?" asked Tony.

"Okay, everyone, let's calm down," said Gwen. "Let's hear what Dr. Rosen has to say."

"Thank you, Mrs. Crenshaw," said the doctor. "Trey is stable right now. He did give us a pretty good scare, but he's resting fine right now."

"Can I take my baby home?" asked Rose.

"No, he can't leave yet. He will have to spend a few days at the hospital. He is doing a lot better, but he is not out of the woods just yet. Trey is still extremely weak and will need a lot of rest. He's a strong-willed young man, so I'm sure he'll make a full recovery. However, a few of his organs are enlarged, so we need to keep him here for treatment and observation."

"He will be better off here," said Tony, as he put his arm around Rose's waist. "He's weak from the episode he just went through, and he needs to rest." Rose wiped the tears from her face and nodded in agreement.

"I want to spend the night here with him," said Rose. "Is that allowed, Dr. Rosen?"

"Of course, it is," replied the doctor. "He will most likely sleep through the night. But if he doesn't, it would be good to have a familiar face close by."

"We'll both stay," said Tony.

"Excellent", said the doctor. "He is being assigned a room as we speak. I will make sure that another recliner and blanket are placed in his room for you two."

"Thank you," said Rose.

"The rest of you might as well go home and get some rest," said Dr. Rosen. "Trey will most likely sleep the rest of the night."

"Thanks, doc, I think we all can use some sleep," said Gwen. "John, you look beat. Let's go home."

"I think I will walk a little," said John. "You go on home."

"Come on, John," pleaded Gwen, "I know you're tired, and we're a pretty good distance from home. You're not as young as you used to be. We need to go home and get some rest so that we can visit Trey tomorrow before we go to The W.O.R.D. event. I hope you are still going with me."

John said nothing about the event. "I'll be okay." I'll call a cab if I get tired," said John.

"I'll give you a ride," said Rev. We know you like to walk when you have a lot on your mind, so what if I take you halfway home? You can walk the rest of the way. You would still get in a couple of miles at least."

"That would make me feel better," said Gwen, "as long as you keep your doctor appointment next week."

"Okay, okay," said John. "I will agree to that. Let's go, Rev."

"I hope you find it in your heart to pray while you're walking," said Gwen. "I hope you thank God for sparing our grandson tonight."

"Our grandson still has a long way to go. Where is God? I really would like to talk to him."

Gwen watched John as he left with his players. Her heart ached as much for her husband as it did for her grandson. Gwen said goodbye to Rose and Tony and left the hospital. As she walked to the car, she could not help but think about what John had just said. Before she pulled off, Gwen closed her eyes and clutched the steering wheel tight with both hands and prayed. Maybe, just maybe, what John had just said in anger and frustration was the answer. Gwen prayed that God would speak to John.

CHAPTER 9

CONFIRMATION

Simon was taken directly to an interrogation room by Lieutenant Perkins. He was instructed to sit at a table and face a mirror that was on a wall directly across from him. As the Lieutenant left the room, he told Simon that he would be back in a few minutes. Simon waited patiently, looking around the empty room. He glanced past the mirror and then quickly turned his head back and stared directly into it as if he noticed something.

It was a two-way mirror, and Simon could see Lieutenant Perkins and two other officers through the glass. He watched them as they looked at him. This went on for a while, and the officers wondered why Simon stared continuously into the mirror. They thought something was wrong with him. Suddenly one of the officers noticed that Simon seemed to be watching them.

"I think he can see us," said Officer Patroski.

"That's impossible," barked the Lieutenant.

"I'm telling you," said Patroski, "he's watching every move we make. Jimmy, walk over to the door as if you are about to leave, then come back over here." Officer Humphries did as Patroski instructed. As Humphries walked, Simon's head turned and followed him to the door. On his way back, Simon's head turned and followed him back to his seat.

"What did I tell you," said Patroski.

They looked bewildered. Each one of them continued to test Simon by moving around the room and pointing at him. Each time, Simon followed their motions with his eyes. He shocked them when he pointed in their direction and motioned for one of them to come to him. Officer Humphries pointed at himself as if to be asking Simon if he wanted him. He shook his head no and pointed to Lieutenant Perkins. The Lieutenant couldn't believe what he was seeing. He sprung from his seat and stormed out of the room.

Officers Humphries and Patroski watched the Lieutenant as he entered the room where Simon was being held. He immediately looked over at the mirror, checking to see if he could see through it. He could not. Officers Humphries and Patroski started making faces at the Lieutenant, testing him to see if he could see them. He made no indication that he could.

"Are you ready to talk to me and tell me where the blood on your hands came from?" asked the Lieutenant. He did not sit down because he did not believe Simon was ready to talk. He had planned to wait a while longer before coming back to the room, but he had to check out the mirror to see if it was defective.

"Why did you tell me that you would be right back, then go into that room and stare at me like an animal in a cage for thirty minutes?" Simon asked.

The Lieutenant wasn't expecting the question, so he stayed on the offensive. "I'm the one asking the questions. Where did the blood come from?"

"I told you where it came from."

"Yes, you said it was the blood of Jesus." An uneasy feeling suddenly came across the Lieutenant. He began to think about the unexplained things that happened every time he was around Simon. First, there was the blackout involving their police cruisers. He later learned that the blackout covered a two-mile radius. Then the darts of the Tasers had no effect on him. Simon simply pulled them from his body. The handcuffs they had put on him mysteriously came off when he was in the cruiser. They didn't even know it until he was getting out of the car. He could have attacked them. Now, he was able to see through a two-way mirror.

"Are you sticking with that lie?" the Lieutenant asked as he slowly placed his hand on his weapon.

"Are you going to fire your weapon at me for telling the truth?"

"No, but I would like to."

"You are a nonbeliever."

"Who in their right mind would believe that the blood on your hands came from a man who supposedly lived over two thousand years ago?"

"I am not referring to the blood on my hands. You do not believe in Jesus Christ."

"What I believe doesn't matter," said the Lieutenant. "What matters is making sure you are punished for your crimes. I can tell that I'm wasting my time with you. I'm going to have you booked and evaluated. Maybe they can get some answers out of you. The lieutenant turned and left the room.

A man and woman came to see Simon five minutes after the lieutenant left the room. One was Pastor Gerald Vincent, and the other was Dr. April Waters. Pastor Vincent was an associate pastor at a local church who did volunteer work at the jail. He happened to be there when Simon was brought in. Lieutenant Perkins asked the pastor to give his opinion on the prisoner since Simon claimed to be an associate of Jesus. Dr. Waters was a psychologist who was on retainer with the city. She was automatically brought in to evaluate any prisoner who appeared to be mentally unstable. They both introduced themselves as they took a seat.

"Interesting," said Simon.

"What is so interesting?" asked Dr. Waters.

"A man of God who covets his neighbor's wife and a doctor who cannot help her child have come to evaluate me."

Dr. Waters and Pastor Vincent were both shocked and a little embarrassed. They looked at each other and then at Simon. They did not know that about each other, and they wondered how Simon knew. Dr. Waters was well known in the community. Her daughter's condition was mentioned in an article about her a couple of years earlier. She was sure Simon had read the article and remembered it. Pastor Vincent could not dismiss Simon's knowledge of his affair so easily. He was noticeably uncomfortable and did all he could to look as if he had no idea what Simon was talking about.

"My daughter's mental challenges were mentioned in an article about me a couple of years ago," said Dr. Waters. "What is your story?"

"My story?" asked Simon. "What are you asking me?"

"Who are you? Where do you come from? Why are you here?" asked Dr. Waters.

"My name is Simon. I am from Cyrene, which is now referred to as Shahhat, Libya. I am here on an assignment."

"Simon who? What is your last name?" the pastor asked after finally recovering from his initial shock.

"I am known only as Simon."

"What is your assignment, and who do you work for?" asked Dr. Waters.

"I am a servant of my Lord and Savior Jesus Christ. My assignment is to win souls to Christ, to spread and protect the gospel, and to keep hope alive."

Lieutenant Perkins and the other two officers were observing Simon, the pastor, and the doctor from the other side of the two-way mirror. "Here we go," said the Lieutenant. "First he claims to be a disciple of Jesus, now he thinks he's Jesse Jackson." The other two officers laughed. "Next he'll claim to be Kris Kringle," said Patroski. They all laughed.

"I hear that you claim the blood on your hands came from Jesus himself. How old do you think you are?" asked Dr. Waters.

Simon suppressed a smile. "If you know the story of Jesus, which

I know that you do, although you don't believe, then you know the answer to that question. Is that the question you will use to determine my mental stability?"

For about ten seconds, Dr. Waters and Simon appeared to be competing in a staring contest. She did not believe he was over two thousand years old. He appeared to be mentally sharp and alert. She dismissed how he knew about her child, but she could not explain how he knew about the pastor's affair. She did not know about it herself, and she assumed it was true based on the pastor's reaction. She would ask him about it later. Pastor Vincent broke the silence.

"Do you consider yourself a disciple of Jesus?"

"More like an apostle," answered Simon.

"Are you familiar with Scripture?" asked the pastor.

"I am."

"Then you know," began the pastor, "that one of the Ten Commandments states that you should not bear false witness against your neighbor, and another says that you should not lie. You seem to be doing both in one statement. That type of behavior would make someone unworthy to be an apostle of Christ."

"This is true, and I would agree," said Simon, "if I was lying. Refusing to believe the truth does not make it a lie. Another one of the Ten Commandments states that you should not commit adultery. That type of behavior would make someone unworthy to be a pastor."

"Ding, ding, round one goes to the convict," laughed Officer Humphries.

"This may be more entertaining than I thought," said Lieutenant Perkins. "Patroski, you should have fixed popcorn." Patroski settled into his chair as they all laughed. "Let's see if the pastor can make a comeback," said the Lieutenant.

Pastor Vincent felt as if he had been slapped in the face. He no longer felt embarrassed, but he felt as if he was under attack. He decided to retaliate.

"In the sixth chapter of Luke, Jesus said 'do not judge, and you will not be judged.'"

"A few verses down, Jesus asked if a blind man could guide a blind man."

"You seem pretty arrogant for a holy man," said the pastor. In the sixteenth chapter of Proverbs, it reads, 'The Lord detests all the proud of heart. Be sure of this: They will not go unpunished.'"

"I could say the same about you, replied Simon, but I prefer to direct you to the twenty-eighth chapter of Proverbs, verse twenty-six specifically, which reads, 'He who trusts in himself is a fool, but he who walks in wisdom is kept safe.'"

The pastor could see that he was not making any progress. Simon seemed to know the Bible as well as he did, if not better. He decided to try a different approach. Dr. Waters had been listening intently to the conversation between Simon and the pastor, and she was amazed at Simon's cognitive abilities. He showed no signs of being mentally unstable. In fact, he appeared to be just the opposite. He appeared to be quite stable and educated.

The pastor and Dr. Waters had both been informed about the unexplained occurrences that seemed to follow Simon. They had been told about the blackout and him being able to see through the two-way mirror. The pastor was still wondering how Simon knew about his affair. He had fought the temptation for a long time and had just succumbed a week ago. He wanted to hear Simon's explanation of the occurrences.

"OK, you have proven that you are familiar with Scripture. However, a few of the officers believe that you have certain powers, or abilities, that cannot be explained. They told me about the darkness that fell when they were about to arrest you, about the Taser darts that had no effect on you, and about a few other things. How do you explain those things? How did you accomplish those feats?

"I find your question very interesting. You do not believe the blood on my hands is the blood of Jesus, but yet you believe I have certain unexplainable powers. To answer your question read

Philippians 4:13," said Simon.

"Is that it? Is that all you have to say?"

"What does that passage of Scripture say?" asked Dr. Waters.

"It says, 'I can do all things through Christ who strengthens me.'"

"Interesting," said Dr. Waters.

"I believe it to be more of evading the question," said the pastor.

"O ye of little faith," said Simon.

"Tell us why we should believe you," said Pastor Vincent. "Why should we believe that you are over two thousand years old and lived during the time of Jesus? First of all, there is no documented character in the Bible that lived to be two thousand years old. Second, if what you say is true, then that means you were one of the Romans who beat Jesus before he was crucified. If that's the case, then you are guilty of murder or of being an accomplice at least. There are no other characters mentioned in the Bible who would have the blood of Jesus on them. I guess you're going to tell us that you're an individual from that time who was not mentioned in the Bible?"

All of a sudden Dr. Waters looked as if she had seen a ghost. She turned pale, and her breathing became more labored. Her heart started to beat a little faster as she and Simon made eye contact. A feeling came across her that she could not explain.

"I will tell you no such thing," said Simon. "I will say that I am disappointed in you for the second time. A pastor that commits adultery and does not remember a very important passage of scripture needs to spend more time reading the bible and praying. Satan has heavily influenced you. By the look on her face, I believe the doctor can give you the answer you are seeking."

Pastor Vincent looked at Dr. Waters, wondering what Simon was talking about. He saw the puzzled look on her face. A tear rolled down her left cheek, but she quickly wiped it away. The pastor never saw it, but Simon did.

"What is he talking about Dr. Waters?"

"There is scripture in the bible that refers to him," said the doctor.

"He appears to be a minor character in the life of Jesus, but scripture actually refers to him by name. I'm surprised you don't recall it. He said that he is Simon of Cyrene. According to the Bible, Simon of Cyrene was the man who helped Jesus carry his cross."

Pastor Vincent quickly looked back at Simon. "You're claiming to be that Simon!"

"I am that Simon," he replied.

"The Bible doesn't mention anything about Simon placing his hands on Jesus," said the pastor.

"The bible doesn't explain why I was selected either," said Simon. "Remember, man wrote the Bible through divine intervention, but every minute of the life of Jesus was not recorded."

"But how?" asked the pastor. "How can you possibly be that Simon? How have you lived so long?"

"For the third time, Pastor, I am disappointed in you. You have heard it many times and have preached on it on several occasions. Apparently, you do not really believe that there is power in the blood!"

After a few seconds of looking deep into Simon's eyes, the pastor rose from his seat and quickly left the room. Simon turned his attention to Dr. Waters. She continued to stare at him in disbelief. Tears flowed down each cheek as she slowly stood to her feet. She wiped her face and slowly turned to leave.

"Your head and your training are telling you that I am a liar, but your heart knows the truth about me," said Simon. "Listen to your heart." Dr. Waters turned and took one last look at Simon before leaving the room.

A few moments later Patroski and Humphries came into the room. They escorted Simon out to have him processed into the system. They snapped his mug shot, took his fingerprints, and thoroughly searched Simon. Simon was forced to remove his clothes and wear an orange jumpsuit. He hated every second of it, but Jesus commanded him to be obedient and to comply with the officers' instructions, and he did.

Simon was locked in a small cell by himself, but he could hear others nearby. He heard a little bit of truth among a bunch of lies. He heard their claims of innocence and injustice, their bravado and bosting, their stories of unbelievable courage while facing impossible odds. He heard the chatter of the guilty, and the tears of the innocent. He sat quietly, prayed, and meditated.

He had been in the cell for less than an hour when two officers entered. One told him to hold his hands out and then handcuffed him. The other officer grabbed Simon by his elbow and led him to another part of the jail. They went up a few floors on the elevator and exited into what was an administrative area. Simon was surprised by all the cameras mounted away from the inmate population. It seemed to him as if those who enforced the law did not trust one another. They turned left and walked down a short hallway. Then they entered the forensic laboratory.

As they entered the lab, they were met by Dr. Albert Singh, who was one of two licensed forensic scientists employed by the police department. Dr. Singh was going to examine the blood on Simon's hands and wrists to see if it matched the blood of any unsolved crimes. The officers took Simon to a nearby table and told him to sit in the only chair that was at the table. They removed his handcuffs from one wrist and fastened it to a ring made into a very heavy table, which was secured to the floor.

"You are going to cooperate. Aren't you, Simon?" asked one of the officers. "We won't have to hold you down; will we?"

"My name is Dr. Singh, and I am going to take a sample of the blood on your hands and wrists. It will sting a little as I collect the sample, but it will be relatively painless," said the doctor.

"There will be no need to restrain me," said Simon as he looked at the officers.

"We'll be back when the doctor finishes," said one of the officers. "Don't get any wild ideas because we'll be close by." Both officers left the room.

Dr. Singh approached Simon with a small glass dish and a small razor-sharp scalpel. He sat the dish down and took the scalpel out of its sheath. Dr. Singh grabbed Simon's left hand with his left hand, as he positioned the scalpel with his right hand.

"Be very still," instructed the doctor as he began to remove a thin layer of skin.

"What is the purpose of this?" asked Simon.

"I need to take a close look at this blood and determine its origin. I will do that by studying the DNA in the samples I take from your hand."

"I know they told you my story, so you know where the blood came from."

"I know where you say it came from, but that is impossible. I have a microscope connected to a computer across the room. I will look at the blood through that microscope and catalog it. The computer will tell me if it matches the blood of any victims who are already in our database."

"How close of a look will you take?"

"Very close," said the doctor. I will look into the cell structure and the nucleus of the blood."

"I wouldn't do that if I were you," said Simon.

"Why is that?"

"Because that is the blood of Jesus, and you will not survive the observation."

"Will not survive the observation?" asked the doctor. "I will just be looking at a blood sample. I do this every day. Why are you being so ominous?"

"I am not trying to scare you. I am trying to save your life. No one has ever seen the face of God. There is a reason for that. The reason is that man cannot survive looking at the face of God in all his glory. If you cannot survive looking at his face, how do you plan to survive looking at the DNA of our creator? Your disbelief will be your downfall."

"Thanks, but I'll be fine." The doctor placed a couple of skin samples into the glass dish and walked over to the microscope. He pulled up a stool and sat down. He removed a couple of microscope slides from a box and set a small skin sample on one of them. He placed a second slide on top of the first one, sealing the sample between them. He secured the slides under the lens of the microscope and began to type on the computer, looking for his cataloged blood samples. When the doctor found what he was looking for, he placed his eye on the microscope and began adjusting the view.

The doctor was in awe at what he saw. He kept magnifying the view, looking closer and closer. All of a sudden, Dr. Singh raised straight up from the microscope. Flames shot from both of his eye sockets, and he and the stool fell straight back to the floor. The flames died out, and black smoke rose from both eye sockets.

"Release me," said Simon, and the handcuffs popped open. "I tried to warn you," said Simon as he walked over to the doctor.

Simon went over to the glass dish on the table, next to the microscope. He placed his left hand next to it, and the skin samples grafted perfectly back to his hand. He took the slides off the microscope and separated them. The skin sample that was on the slide also grafted perfectly back to Simon's left hand. He spoke a few words and his orange jumpsuit became a casual pull-over shirt, a pair of jeans, and a jacket. Simon left the lab and the hospital without being noticed and blended into the night.

CHAPTER 10

THE MEETING

John, Ezekiel, and a couple of the other ball players rode down Bardstown Road in silence. The ball players were talking, but John was preoccupied. Every so often he would give his opinion on whatever they were discussing, but for the most part, he just gazed out of his window in deep thought. Ezekiel looked over at his coach a few times as he drove and tried to take John's mind off of his grandson by asking him some basketball-related questions, but it did little good. John always replied with short responses that left little room to continue the conversation. Ezekiel knew when to pull back.

The players had gotten the hint that John didn't feel like talking. Ezekiel focused on the road while the two players in the back seat talked softly to each other. Ezekiel knew John's story well and felt bad for his coach. The whole team, in fact, the entire school, knew the story of how much John had struggled when his son died twenty years earlier. Two years after his son died, John's team won their first state basketball championship. The local newspaper dedicated an entire section of the paper to the players and their coach. The story about the coach compared John's biggest loss to his biggest victory. John dedicated the championship season to his son. That article seemed to resurface at least once every year.

The players were really concerned about their coach when they heard that his grandson was suffering from the same ailment that his son had. They all gathered in the locker room after practice, with the assistant coaches, and prayed for healing for Trey. John knew about it, but he never attended.

"You can let me out up here on the next block," said John.

Ezekiel pulled the car over to the right shoulder, slowly came to a stop, and put the car in park. John got out of the vehicle, but before he could shut the door, one of the players from the back seat got out and moved into the front passenger seat.

"See you, Coach," said Ezekiel and the other two players.

"Thanks, Rev," said John, "I'll see you guys at practice on Monday."

"See you at practice, coach," replied Ezekiel.

Ezekiel let John out further from his home than what they had previously agreed on. He didn't say anything because he knew that John needed this time to himself. John was about three miles from his house at this point. Ezekiel pulled the car away from the curve and sped off. John managed a slight smile as he watched Rev's personalized license plate fade into the night.

John zipped his jacket up, put his hands in his pockets, and began walking at a swift pace. There was a slight breeze, so he raised his collar, lowered his head a little, and returned his hands to his pocket. He paced himself to keep from overexerting. He did that unconsciously sometimes when he was upset or angry, although it hadn't happened in a while. Lately, he had been feeling pretty good and was able to increase his pace and distance without tiring as fast as he used to. Tonight's walk was farther still but not by much. He looked at his watch to see how long it would take him to get home. For some reason, despite his condition, his endurance was getting better.

Though he tried to concentrate on his health, to take his mind off Trey, it didn't last very long. He felt helpless, not quite as bad as when Junior was sick but still helpless. He blamed himself for Junior's death, and Trey's suffering because he was the carrier of this deadly disease.

It was one reason for his health concerns. It had taken his son from him, and now it was threatening to take his grandson. There were some days he wanted to curse his parents for passing this gene on to him, but he never really got a chance to know them. He asked himself almost every day why his life had been so hard and why he could not be happy.

"Your happiness does not depend on your circumstances," said Simon.

John came to a dead stop and looked around. He did not see anyone. He thought that he was either hearing things or going crazy, or maybe both. The voice was clear and distinct and addressed exactly what he had been thinking. He thought that his mind was playing tricks on him, so he slowly kept walking.

"Happiness is a choice, and you choose not to be happy."

Again, John stopped and looked around. He turned around in a complete circle, searching in the darkness for the voice he just heard so clearly. He dropped his head and closed his eyes. He tried to rationalize what had just happened. Somehow, I am unconsciously answering my own thoughts he reasoned. Yes, the voice is only in my head. No one was out here talking to him, he reasoned.

"I must be more stressed than I thought," John whispered to himself. "Trey's illness is really taking its toll on me."

"John Samuel Crenshaw, you are a hurt and confused man."

John quickly opened his eyes and raised his head. Simon was standing directly in front of him, about ten feet away. John looked Simon up and down. He instantly noticed Simon's red hands and, like most people, assumed that they were the result of a heinous crime. He was wondering how this tall, muscular, black man knew his name, what he wanted with him, and who he had harmed. John recalled that he was a teenager the last time he had a physical altercation with anyone, but he would go down swinging if this guy was up to no good.

"Relax, John," said Simon. "I am not here to hurt you, and my hands are not red for the reasons you are thinking."

"Who are you?" asked John, "and how do you know what I am thinking?"

"My name is Simon, and I know all about you."

"How is that possible? I have never seen you before in my life. What do you want with me?"

"I am here to help you."

"Help me with what? I haven't asked anyone for help."

"You asked God to spare your grandson."

A cold chill raced through John's body as he and Simon glared intently at each other. That is the last thing he had expected to hear. John didn't know what to think. He had not prayed in front of anyone since Junior died, which was over twenty years ago, and they were silent prayers. His prayers for Trey had been earlier that very day, but they were not spoken aloud. He promised himself that if Trey didn't beat this disease he would never pray again. How can this guy know about his prayers and about him and his grandson? John reasoned that this man recognized him as a local high school basketball coach and knew of his story. He probably just assumed that he had prayed for Trey. Though his heart was racing, John's demeanor became calmer.

"I don't have time for these games," said John. "I need to get on my way." John continued walking and cautiously watched Simon as he passed by him. Simon spoke once more after John had walked by.

"It was less than an hour ago that you told your wife that you want to speak to God. He is listening to you."

John stopped but did not turn around. He took a few more steps and then stopped again, and slowly turned around to face Simon.

"Are you claiming to be God?"

"No, I am a servant of Jesus Christ who has told me all about you. Jesus has sent me here to help you."

"If that is true, you would not be here with me. You would be at the hospital healing my grandson or at least praying for him because you don't look as if you're in the healing business. I don't know what asylum you escaped from or why you think you know me but leave me alone and let me be on my way. If Jesus is real, I'm sure he would have sent someone more qualified than you to represent him."

"You don't believe that."

"What are you talking about?"

"You said if Jesus is real as if you doubt that he is. As I said a minute ago, you are hurt and confused. That's why I am here."

"And why again are you here?"

"I am here to restore your faith and your trust in Jesus and to hopefully ease your pain a little."

"Good luck with that," said John. "You can start by being straight up with me and telling me who you are and how you know me."

"I will tell you, but you won't believe me. I am Simon, known to most of the world as Simon of Cyrene. I helped Jesus carry his cross on his march to his crucifixion. That is where the blood on my hands came from. It is the blood of Jesus. He repaid my kindness by allowing me to personally serve him. Although you try to deny Jesus, I know that you know the bible."

"You're claiming to be Simon of Cyrene, the guy in the bible who helped Jesus over two thousand years ago? You want me to believe you're that Simon?"

"That is who I am."

"That's impossible."

"Is it impossible that I know about you giving your cross to the young accident victim who lost his father on the same day that your son died? You gave the young boy the cross that your grandmother had given you, which you loved second only to your family. You're the one who called the hospital and informed them of the accident. How is it possible that I know about that incident when you have told no one about it, not even your wife?"

John was stunned. He was speechless. He didn't know what to say. This man was right; he had not told anyone about his involvement in that accident. John was starting to feel a little nervous but not from fear. For a split second, he thought that maybe this guy was actually who he said he was.

"Nothing is impossible with Jesus," said Simon, "but you know that. You have survived a lot of heartaches in your life. You should be praising Jesus for bringing you through them, instead of trying to convince yourself that he doesn't exist."

"You're right. I have survived a lot of heartaches, but I'm not looking forward to dealing with the death of my grandson. I don't know if I can survive if he died. Jesus wasn't with me during my most difficult times. He abandoned me during those times."

"You can't believe that," said Simon.

"Why shouldn't I believe it? None of my prayers were answered during those times."

"You don't realize how blessed and protected you are, do you?"

"No, I guess I don't," said John. "Why don't you tell me about it?"

"Both of your parents died in a car accident when you were very young. As a matter of fact, your situation was similar to the young child who you assisted twenty years ago, except that young child still had his mother."

"Don't remind me."

"You were heart-broken, of course," said Simon, "but if you remember, you begged your parents to allow you to go with them. Your maternal grandmother agreed to watch you while they were gone. They were going away for a long weekend, and you would have had to miss a couple of days of school. They didn't want you to miss your classes. They promised to make it up to you by taking you on a nice vacation during the summer. If you had been with them, you, too, would have died that day. That is the first time that Jesus intervened on your behalf."

"I don't know who you are," said John, "or how you know all of this, but I have often wished I had been with my parents. I often wish that we would have perished together as a family. It would have saved me a lot of heartaches."

"I'm sure that many people have told you that you are lucky that you weren't with your parents on the trip. You've probably heard that more times than you care to remember. However, it wasn't luck, it was divine intervention. You are highly favored and have been surrounded by guardian angels your entire life."

John looked at Simon through squinty eyes as if to be questioning his last statement.

"I know you find that hard to believe, but it's true. Your grandmother played a big part in your development. She became your legal guardian and raised you after your parents passed away."

"What's your point?" asked John.

"Your grandmother made sure that you had a Christian foundation. She took you to church and helped you to know and understand the gospel. Though you try to convince yourself, and others, that you are not familiar with the bible, we both know that you know it better than most. What you didn't know, until later in life, is how seriously ill your grandmother was when she became your guardian.

Just a couple of weeks before your parents died, your grandmother was given only three months to live. She convinced your parents to leave for that long weekend so that she could spend some time with her favorite grandchild before she passed. Your parents purposefully planned to leave during a time when you were scheduled to be in school so that they could use school as an excuse for you to not go along. They had always emphasized how important school was to you, and they knew you would be disappointed but would believe their reason for having you stay behind. They asked your aunt, your father's oldest sister, to check on you and your grandmother while they were out of town, just in case your grandmother had a medical emergency."

"I remember Aunt Pat and other family members being around a lot when my parents died. To me, it was normal for my family to call and to stop by often to support me after that horrible accident. All families do that, we look after each other."

"True, that is how it is supposed to be. However, you didn't know about all the conversations and arguments that took place between your grandmother and other members of your family."

"What arguments? What are you talking about?"

"The other members of your family did not want your grandmother to be your guardian because of her illness. She had already been given a death sentence, so to speak, and they did not want you to go through another traumatic loss in your young life. Your Uncle Joseph wanted to take you to live with him, and the rest of the family agreed. He had a couple of children, and everyone, except your grandmother, thought it best if you were raised with your cousins, who were similar in age."

"They were okay, but I always felt out of place around them. They were doing very well, and they always let you know how well off they were."

"Your grandmother knew this. She was a very committed believer, and she knew that your Uncle Joseph's family never attended church. He felt that he was a self-made man and that he reached financial freedom from his own efforts and intelligence. Your grandmother wanted to make sure that you knew who your Lord and Savior is. She felt bad for convincing your parents into taking that weekend get-away, and she wanted to make sure you were raised properly. Through divine intervention, she was able to convince the rest of your family to allow you to stay with her. She promised to give up her guardianship the moment her doctors said that she was no longer able to care for you. What your family didn't know was that through prayer, God promised your grandmother that she would see your twenty-fifth birthday."

"My grandmother died when I was twenty-seven."

"Yes, you were twenty-seven years and three months of age when your grandmother was called to her heavenly home. She lived approximately twenty years longer than her doctors estimated. Even when you found out that your grandmother was sick, you had no idea how long she had been sick. You didn't realize that Jesus commanded the cancer to be still and didn't allow it to move until twenty years later."

"How can that be true?" asked John. "That can't be true. Granny Ethel never looked sick. She never acted as if she was sick. She was full of energy for her age. Granny Ethel played ball with me. I owe everything to her."

"Yes, she did play ball with you. She got you interested in basketball to take your mind off your loss and to keep you out of the streets. She also used basketball as a proverbial carrot, dangling it in your face to keep you on track. She'd tell you that if you didn't keep your grades up and didn't go to church, you wouldn't be able to play basketball

"She would take basketball away from me," said John. She made me sit out my entire sophomore year when my grades started to suffer. She told me that my coach didn't want a dumb ballplayer who couldn't learn the plays. Actually, my coach got angry and pleaded with Granny Ethel to allow me to play. I had a really good freshman year, and he was counting on me being available my sophomore year."

"That's when your grandmother made you concentrate on your grades and the Bible. You made huge strides in your schoolwork and understanding of the gospel. Your whole character and demeanor changed. You became so much more mature, and your grandmother loved the person you were becoming. She never had any more problems with you in school or at church. That year away from basketball made you hungrier. It made you work harder. You developed your skills far beyond your coach's expectations. You became the star of a team that was blessed with other great athletes."

"We won the state championship two in a row. I was recruited by every major college in the country. I loved my hometown, so I stayed home and played for the University of Louisville. We were doing well during my senior year until I got a career-ending injury. I was projected as a first-round draft pick before the accident. I prayed night and day that the doctors were wrong. I prayed that I could continue playing basketball, but it didn't happen. For five years, I tried to rehabilitate myself, but my knee wasn't strong enough to pass the NBA physical exam. Though my knee felt fine, I was told it was permanently damaged. I would be able to live a normal life, but my knee would never be able to endure the wear and tear of professional ball. My pain and suffering doubled when my grandmother died, just after my last NBA rejection. I felt as if I had been stabbed in my heart twice. I prayed, but my prayers were not answered. Where was Jesus then?"

"Your story is missing some very important facts," said Simon. "Your prayers were answered, but you have to be careful what you ask for. Like most people, you conveniently forgot about the promises you made to God. You remember only what you asked for but did not receive. Your knee injury was one of the worse ever recorded. It was so bad there was talk of amputating your left leg because of a loss of circulation. You remember Dr. Ludwig Kronin, don't you?"

"Of course, I do. He's the one who saved my leg."

"At the time, he was the world's top orthopedic surgeon, who specialized in knee surgery and reconstruction. He was in town for a sports injury conference and was rightfully presented as the featured speaker. Your coach was able to get a note to him before he left town, informing him of your injury and prognosis of amputation. Your coach pleaded with him to take a look at your knee before he left town. As you stated, you were predicted as a top draft pick, and he had read about your injury in the local paper.

He agreed to take a look at your knee. Dr. Kronin was able to reconstruct your knee and save your leg. Everybody was telling you how lucky you were that the top orthopedic surgeon in the country, who specialized in exactly what you needed, happened to be in town when you suffered your injury. That was not luck, John. That was divine planning.

There is no such thing as luck. That is a word created by man to explain the things he cannot understand. Luck is a two-sided coin, with miracle written on the other side. Miracle is another word created by man to explain the things he cannot understand, but at least miracles are attributed to God. The funny thing is that God doesn't believe in miracles, because he can do anything. As I told you before, you are highly favored and are protected under direct order from Jesus. Give credit to Him, not to luck."

"However, when you first heard that the doctors were planning to amputate your leg, you prayed like you had never prayed before and like you have never done since. You were stronger in your faith then, and your prayers were so sincere. You promised God that you would find a way to serve him until you die if he spared your leg. You said that you didn't think that you were cut out to be a minister and that you didn't care if you ever played basketball again. You said that you just wanted to be made whole. You wanted to keep both of your legs and be able to walk and live a normal life."

"When Dr. Kronin's operation was successful, your aspirations of playing professional basketball returned. You forgot about your promise to God. You were determined to work hard and train hard to rehabilitate your knee. To this day, you have never given another thought to serving God. You wanted to stay close to basketball, so Jesus used basketball as the way in which you could fulfill your promise. Though you do not participate in the team prayers anymore, you don't stop your players and assistant coaches from praying before and after games. Whether you want to admit it or not, that is a sign of approval. Your prayer was answered, but your promise was forgotten."

John could do nothing but stare. Everything Simon had just said was true. As Simon spoke, everything started to come back to him as clear as crystal. He started to feel a little ashamed of himself because he had forgotten about his promise to God. He had not given much thought to the team prayers, but when he thought about it, that was true too. He didn't mind his team or his assistant coaches praying before or after games. John was having mixed emotions. His grandmother's teachings started coming back to him.

"As far as your grandmother goes, her prayers were answered. She wanted to stay well enough to raise you and give you the biblical foundation she wanted you to have. She was very proud of the man you had become. Your grandmother suffered as much as you did when your basketball career ended. She wanted you to have what you had worked so hard for. When you examine your life, you will realize that Jesus has been there for you every step of the way. Stop blaming God for the difficult times you have endured. God carried you through those difficult times."

"I don't know how you know all of this about me, but everything you have said is true," said John. "It's hard to believe you are who you say you are. You're right. I do know the bible, and I know the power that the blood of Jesus is supposed to have. However, bloody hands and all, it doesn't change the fact that my son was laid in his grave as an innocent child who never did anything to anyone, and my grandson is fighting for his life. If you want me to regain my faith in God, then tell Jesus to heal my grandson and convince me that my son's death was necessary to make this a better world. Then and only then will I know that Jesus is real."

John's eyes filled with tears as he turned and continued his walk home. He had not shed tears since his son had died. He had not been so outwardly emotional since then either. Whatever just happened, he was sure he would wake up tomorrow and realize that it was all just a dream. He could hear Simon speaking to him very clearly as he walked, but John was not interested in further conversation.

"John, you know the story of how sin entered the world. Death, pain, and suffering are all part of the package. Everyone must die unless they're caught up in the rapture. No one, not even me, knows when we will be called home. You know the urgency of the gospel. Very few people are prepared for the death of a child, and fewer ever consider it will happen to them. Due to his innocence, your son will spend eternity with Christ. Jesus has heard your request, but the restoration of your faith is necessary for your survival. The healing of your grandson will depend on your faith."

John stopped in his tracks when he heard this. Why would the healing of his grandson depend on his faith? John turned around to ask Simon that very question, but he was not there. John looked all around, but Simon was nowhere in sight. He stood there contemplating Simon's last statement. Jesus doesn't negotiate with us for our faith, he thought, and he quickly dismissed that idea. He also refused to believe that Trey's life was in his hands. He knew without a doubt that he would do anything within his power to save his grandson, even if it meant sacrificing his own life. He continued his walk home, reliving every word of his conversation with Simon.

"Thank you, Jesus," whispered Simon. "Thank you for placing John's story in my mouth, and for reminding him of a long-forgotten promise. I believe you have his attention once again."

CHAPTER 11

THE W.O.R.D.

The day had finally come, and Louisville, Kentucky, had become the news media capital of the world. Every country in the world was represented in the city. The W.O.R.D. would be broadcast to every location on the planet that had the technology to receive it. Ninety percent of the world's nearly eight billion people would have access to the live broadcast. Thirty-second commercials during this event averaged slightly over sixty million dollars, which was more than ten times the cost of a similar commercial aired during the Super Bowl. Though both the Super Bowl and the W.O.R.D. were broadcast live for roughly three and a half hours, commercials aired only twenty-five percent as often during the W.O.R.D. as they did during the Super Bowl. The price had a lot to do with that.

Traffic in Louisville was chaotic, as it had been the entire week leading up to the event. Twenty-four hours before the event an automobile was almost useless in downtown Louisville. You could walk a mile before you could drive a hundred yards. There were so many tents along the side of most roads that Louisville, and parts of southern Indiana, looked like a homeless camp. The visitors who had been fortunate enough to drive into the city parked their vehicles on streets as close as they could and then walked to downtown Louisville. They set up tents near the venue where the conference was being held.

Law enforcement spent a couple of days before the start of the event to clear and block off these streets so that the event participants and first responders if needed, could get to the venue.

Louisville had become a security nightmare. Law enforcement had been very visible all week, but their number had doubled on this day. There were almost as many plain-clothed officers as there were uniformed ones. Yet, they still didn't feel adequately staffed for an event of this size.

The event started at 7:00 p.m., but the doors opened at 5:00 p.m. Some of the ticket holders start lining up as early as noon, even though they had an assigned seat. The sensible ticket holders, like John and Gwen, planned to leave early enough to maneuver through the madness and arrive at their seat at a reasonable time.

As Gwen got dressed, she tried to make small talk with John, but it was useless. He either gave her short, one-word answers or didn't answer at all. Gwen thought that he was upset with her for pleading with him to go to this event. She wanted him to join her, but she wouldn't have been upset if he decided not to attend. She knew how hard he was taking Trey's sickness and how fragile he was. John wasn't upset though; he was just preoccupied with the conversation he had had with Simon the night before.

He had not told her about his encounter with Simon, but that encounter was why he decided to go to the W.O. R. D. As he got dressed, John could not get the conversation he had with Simon out of his head. He was feeling guilty because he had forgotten about the promise he had made to God. He hoped that going to the event with Gwen would make him feel as if he was doing something that God approved of.

In reality, John had no interest in the W.O.R.D. event, but his guilt was causing him stress. He was sincere when he made the promise to God so many years ago, and he couldn't for the life of him figure out how he had changed so much. He knew that the disappointments and difficulties of life had everything to do with who he had become, but that is all counter to the teachings of Christ. Somewhere along the way Satan had found his weakness and had stolen his joy. The more he thought about it, the worse he felt, because his grandmother would be so disappointed in him. He thought about how much she had sacrificed and how she had hidden the sickness from him. Yet, he could not ever remember her feeling sorry for herself or showing any indication that her faith had diminished or waivered for a second.

John suddenly had a revelation. Everyone had paid so much attention to him when his parents died that he never considered how his grandmother felt about losing a child. How could he have not thought about that? Of course, she never spoke of it. She was so busy trying to console him, provide for him, and stay strong for him that she suppressed her own grief to see to his needs. John hadn't given his wife as much comfort and consoling as he should have either. She tried to console him, but he did not do the same for her. She had lost a child too. He felt like such a self-centered hypocrite. He wanted to cry, but he didn't. As they were leaving out the house, John gave his wife a big hug and a kiss and told her that he loved her. This set Gwen's mood for the rest of the night, and she returned his expressions of love. At that moment, she felt hopeful for her husband. She knew that he was battling some internal demons, but she felt like he might be up for some light conversation.

"Have you heard about the earthquake and tsunami that are expected to hit Japan sometime tonight?" Gwen asked.

"No, I haven't," replied John. "Do they think it's going to be bad?"

"It's expected to be bad, worse than the 2011 tsunami that hit northeastern Japan. The news channel squeezed the story in before talking about the twenty-four-hour coverage of the W.O.R.D. The ironic part is, the quake is in almost the same area as the 2011 quake."

"Wow," exclaimed John. "I remember that the 2011 quake registered as high as 9.1, and the tsunami that followed had waves over a hundred feet high, killing over twenty thousand people and causing massive destruction."

"The authorities there have been calling for everyone to evacuate the area for the last two days. I just heard about it today. We have to pray for those people, John."

Gwen looked at John after suggesting they should pray for the people of Japan. She hoped he wouldn't take offense. She didn't think about it until the words left her lips. This was a natural thing for her to say because she always talked about praying for others when she heard that someone was in need. Gwen thought that John would ignore her comment and continue doing what he was doing, which was what he usually did. She was surprised when he responded positively.

"I hope the people of Japan are praying for each other," said John, "and praying to the God of Abraham. You know Christianity is not their primary religion."

Gwen held back a smile and did not respond. She did not want to push it, but she was thrilled that he agreed in his own way, without telling her how useless prayer was. She grabbed John's left arm and hugged it as they walked to the car.

They left a little early so that they would have time to stop by the hospital and see Trey. Rose and Tony had come home early that morning to take a shower, change clothes, and return to the hospital. Trey was doing well and was in good spirits. You could see both the joy and the pain on John's face when a couple of nurses told him that Trey asked about his pawpaw. John couldn't help but smile, but the pain was evident in his eyes. He and Gwen spent about thirty minutes at the hospital. They spoke briefly with Rose and Tony but spent most of their time with Trey. The doctor told them that unless he had a major setback, Trey would be going home the next day. Before they left, John and Gwen kissed Trey and told him they would see him at home tomorrow.

"You promise, pawpaw, you promise?" Trey pleaded.

Trey's question caught John by surprise, and it seemed as if time slowed considerably before he answered. All eyes were on John as he made eye contact with Trey, gave him a big smile, and answered his question.

"I promise!" he answered with conviction.

Again, Gwen smiled at John's comment. She was not sure what was going on with him, but she liked it. She did not ask any questions. She wanted to enjoy every minute of it. John was still not the man he was before Junior's sickness was diagnosed, but she could see a huge difference in him within the last twenty-four hours. She would take what she could get. John was again silent as they drove to the event. He was preoccupied, and Gwen could sense it. She did not interrupt his thought process with small talk.

They arrived at the venue in good time. They had to park a couple of miles away but were able to catch a shuttle to the venue. John and Gwen found the shuttle ride to be very comfortable and relaxing. They appreciated the ease and the efficiency of the shuttle service. They boarded about a block from where they parked and were let off right in front of the venue. They had a reasonable wait when they got in line, and they were in their seats within thirty minutes. The event wasn't scheduled to start for another forty-five minutes, and they spent that time in their own way. The time passed quickly for John because he was once again preoccupied with thought. The conversation he had with Simon was still heavy on his mind. Simon made him think about things he had not thought about in a long time, and he felt that he must choose between who he had become and who he wanted to be.

Gwen, on the other hand, was enjoying the entire experience. It had been a while since she and John had been out together. A lot was going on, and she wanted to see and remember all of it. She even enjoyed watching the stagehands finish setting up and testing the microphones. People were steadily streaming in, and the place had almost reached its capacity. Any time she was at a show or event Gwen loved to mingle. She enjoyed meeting and talking to all kinds of people, and this event had drawn people from all walks of life.

It was an international smorgasbord. From her wait in line, to finally reaching her seat, she was able to meet and talk to about a half dozen people. Their conversations were short because everyone was in a hurry to get to their seat, including John. Gwen was thoroughly enjoying herself when all of a sudden, all the lights dimmed, except for those on the stage. It was at that moment that she noticed the large screens hanging from the rafters. There were four of them strategically placed so that no matter where you were sitting you could look at a screen and see what was happening on stage. There were cameras everywhere, covering every angle of the stage and every seat in the venue.

A microphone and stand were placed in the left corner of the stage, near the front. Further back and in the center of the stage was the main setup for the speakers of the event. There was a podium in the middle of the stage with four chairs behind it, two on each side. The stage décor was kept simple, and it looked as if it was set outdoors. There were a lot of plants and flowers and greenery all around, with a backdrop of a bright blue sky, sprinkled with a few clouds. The artificial turf that covered the floor gave the resemblance of grass. A man walked up to the microphone placed at the corner of the stage.

"Good evening ladies and gentlemen. My name is Reed Pierce, and I will be your host this evening. I will be introducing each group tonight right before they come to the stage. Each religious group will tell you a little about their beliefs, their origin, and why they believe what they believe. They will probably try to recruit a few of you with their charm and persuasion, but sometimes their recruiting tactics involve trying to discredit other religions. Please don't take it personally. Before the night is over you will hear a little about the history, traditions, practices, and beliefs of each group. Since Christianity is the largest religion in the world, each group will tell you how their beliefs compare to Christianity."

"The order of appearance was determined by the religion's international ranking. That ranking is based on how many worldwide members each group has. Usually, the religion with the largest number of members chooses to speak last, with the next largest appearing right before them, and so on. Since Christianity is the world's largest religion, the Christians have chosen to appear last. Therefore, we will start with the tenth-largest religion in the world, which is Judaism. It has between fourteen and seventeen million followers worldwide. Judaism is the ethnic religion of the Jews. Its foundational text is called the Torah, which is part of the larger text known as the Tanakh. There is much, much more I can tell you about Judaism, but I prefer to let them enlighten you. Ladies and gentlemen, I present to you the representatives of Judaism."

The Jews came out in their cultural attire and said a prayer, and then all but one of them took a seat. The spokesman went to the podium and explained their beliefs and described why the Jews will inherit the earth and why they were God's chosen people. They spoke for about twenty minutes before the next religious group came onstage.

As promised, Pierce said a little about each group and introduced them before they came to the microphone. This went on for about two hours as the top seven religions gave their presentations. There was a fifteen-minute intermission after the fourth-largest religion, Korean Shamanism, also known as Korean folk religion, left the stage. After the intermission, Pierce appeared once again to introduce the world's third-largest religion.

"The belief of the next group coming to the stage is referred to as Hinduism. Practiced mainly in India, Hinduism is the third-largest religion in the world with over 1.15 billion followers. The dot on their forehead is called a "bindi." It identifies them as being Hindus, and it expresses their spirituality. The bindi is referred to as the third eye and represents spiritual sight. They believe that it allows them to see things that the physical eyes cannot see. Hinduism is widely believed to be the oldest religion in the world. Ladies and gentlemen, coming to the stage are your Hinduism representatives."

As Pierce exited the stage, five Hindus entered from the left of the stage, dressed in their very colorful, loose-fitting native attire. One person went to the microphone, and the other four began to dance in front of the podium. With a very noticeable accent, the man at the microphone began to interpret the dance through song. With a rhythmic voice, his narration was perfectly timed with the moves of the dancers. The dancers, two men, and two women moved effortlessly across the floor. Their singing and dancing continued for eight minutes. The singer joined the dancers during the last thirty seconds of the routine and blended in with them in perfect step without missing a beat. The dance came to a choreographed end, and the audience showed its approval with a round of applause. The singer went back to the podium, and the other four sat down in the chairs behind it.

"Good evening, ladies and gentlemen. My name is Atulya Kumar. What you just witnessed is called a kirtan, which is a religious story told in dance and song. There are many different sects or variations of Hinduism, depending on what part of India you are from. However, all the variations, like all religions, have a common form of devotion or worship. The Hindu word for worship is Bhakti, and we have many different ways to worship. The kirtan is one of many."

"No one single person can be credited with being the founder of Hinduism. Our religion is a fusion of different Indian cultures, philosophies, and traditions. It is the most widely accepted faith in India and has a significant number of followers in the Caribbean, Southeast Asia, North America, Europe, and Africa. Most scholars refer to our beliefs as more of a way of life than a religion. However, our divine god manifests himself in many ways. We believe there is an eternal way of life that all Hindus must follow; it involves such traits as honesty, purity, goodwill, mercy, patience, self-restraint, generosity, and refraining from injuring any living being. Most religions have similar beliefs, but they attribute their beliefs to one person, teacher, or founder. However, like most religions, we believe that a person's basic nature lies within their spirit."

"The Hindus believe that all living things have a spirit and that your spirit is where god resides with you. You see, deep in your spirit you are pure. Deep in your divine spirit, you are full of peace, joy, and wisdom and are forever united with god. Remember, Hinduism is the oldest religion in the world, and most other religions copied off of us. Christianity is the largest religion in the world, based off of membership, but they, too, copied off the Hindus."

A few irritated Christians shouted out their objections. They were tired of the other religions ridiculing and criticizing their beliefs. Atulya Kumar was enjoying the pushback. He stood at the podium smiling, which irritated the boisterous few even more. Kumar raised both arms and hunched his shoulders as if to say it is what it is. As he was looking around, he saw two bright red lights at the top of the center aisle. Kumar made a face as if he recognized the source of the red lights. He suddenly clutched his throat with both hands. The audience thought that he was belittling them by giving the choking sign, and they became more boisterous. In actuality, Kumar had lost his voice. As hard as he tried, he could not speak. Kumar looked back up at the top of the center aisle and saw two red hands disappear into the darkness.

CHAPTER 12

PRAYERS ANSWERED

Tony and Rose were exhausted. It was more of mental fatigue than a physical one. The hospital had brought a second recliner into Trey's room and placed it beside the one that was already there. They were both fully reclined with a blanket covering them. They had been at the hospital since Trey was admitted and were determined not to leave his side, other than the occasional trip home to shower and change clothes. They had just laid down minutes ago after Trey's procedure was completed.

They were relieved to know that his condition had not deteriorated since he was admitted, but they had not seen much improvement. Hopefully, that was only because he was tired from all he had been through. Trey had received a treatment using the blood from Dr. Richards, along with the mixture that had been created from the research of combining Dr. Richards's blood with Junior's blood. Trey was already pretty weak, and the treatment made him even more so. The doctors told Tony and Rose that it would take at least 90 days before they would be able to tell if the treatment was helping. Once he left the hospital, barring any other setbacks, Trey would need to return every 30 days for a checkup and status report on the treatment.

Rose was very familiar with this incurable disease. When she was old enough to read and operate a computer, she learned everything she could about amyloidosis. She knew that it was a rare blood disease in which your bone marrow produced an abnormal protein called an amyloid. This protein couldn't be broken down by the body and could be absorbed into any tissue or organ. Too much buildup of the amyloid protein would cause organ failure. Trey's heart had not been seriously affected, but his kidney, spleen, liver, and nervous system had been.

Though amyloidosis is not a form of cancer, doctors have found some success with chemotherapy. Chemotherapy treatment has helped stop the growth of the abnormal cells that produced the amyloid protein. Doctors often use blood stem cell transplants, in conjunction with the chemotherapy treatment. Some patients, such as Trey, require dialysis to help break up the abnormal protein matter in the blood that the kidneys can't remove. Since amyloidosis can affect your joints, doctors also use anti-inflammatory medicine. Since scientists have not discovered a cure, the main goal of most treatment plans is to slow down the production of the abnormal protein.

After much discussion, Rose and Tony came to an agreement about Trey's treatment plan. They decided to follow the advice of Dr. Rosen. Though Trey's condition had gotten progressively worse over the last year, they were not ready to administer chemo treatments. The experiments using the blood of Dr. Richards had shown some positive results, and they decided to go that route instead. This involved the transplant of stem cells from Dr. Richards's blood, along with the solution made from Junior's blood. They also administered some anti-inflammatory medicine. The procedure started at about 6:00 p.m., right after John and Gwen left, and it took about three hours.

Tony comforted Rose as Trey was going through the treatment. They were allowed to watch, and it looked to be so painful. Although Trey had been put to sleep and didn't feel anything, Rose swore she felt pain when the doctors injected the stem cell solution into Trey's body.

The doctors told Tony and Rose that Trey would probably sleep through the night very comfortably, but he could wake up in pain in the morning. The doctors had given him some pain medicine to help him sleep through the night. Rose and Tony believed their presence would be comforting for him when he awoke in the morning. The doctors warned that Trey would experience some pain and discomfort for a few days after the procedure

Rose was counting on Trey being able to go home the next day. Dr. Rosen had told them it would depend on his vital signs. He had to make sure that Trey did not have a fever and was not having any negative reactions from the stem cell solution. Rose considered them blessed because Dr. Richards's blood matched Trey's. Though Trey still had a port in his arm to administer medicine, he was hooked up to only one machine, to monitor his pulse. The doctor told them it was a good sign if he slept comfortably throughout the night.

It was 10:30 p.m., and Tony and Rose were fast asleep. Rose twisted and turned a bit. She was feeling uncomfortable as if a weight were on her. As she lay on her back, her left arm rested on her stomach, but it felt numb. She couldn't move it. Rose opened her eyes in a bit of panic only to discover that Trey had left his bed and had crawled into her lap. He did this all the time at home after he had played all day and had worn himself out. He would crawl into her lap, and she would carry him to his bed and tuck him in. Acting out of instinct, Rose gathered Trey in her arms and began to get up to take him to his bed.

As her grogginess faded, she then remembered where she was. She wasn't sure if she should be overjoyed or concerned. The doctor said that Trey would sleep through the night, yet here he was in her lap. He said that Trey would experience some pain when he woke up, yet he was not whining or showing any signs of being in pain. He had disconnected the clip-on monitor that was on him, and Rose noticed that the monitor was showing that he didn't have a pulse. She knew a nurse would be in there soon. She stayed as still as she could so that she wouldn't wake him, and she reached over and nudged Tony until he woke up.

"What is it, Baby?" asked Tony. "Is everything okay?"

"I'm not sure," Rose responded. "Take a look."

Tony turned toward Rose to see why she had awakened him. He sat straight up in his recliner when he saw Trey in her lap.

"Honey, why did you take him out of the hospital bed? He was supposed to stay on that monitor."

"I didn't take him out of the bed," explained Rose. "I woke up, and he was in my lap. You know he does this all the time at home. He seems to be fine. He is sleeping comfortably, and he doesn't seem to be in any pain. I want to hold him all night, but he probably should be put back in bed and hooked up to the monitor."

At that time, a nurse rushed into the room. She turned on the light and went straight to Trey's bed. She looked confused when she saw that he was not there. She took a quick glance around the room and found the answer to her question of where he was. She walked over to Rose, took Trey from her, and walked over to the bed. She placed him back in the bed and reconnected him to the monitor. She felt his forehead to see if he had a fever and began to take his pulse. After determining that he was fine, the nurse walked back over to Rose with a scolding look on her face.

"I didn't take him from the bed," said Rose before the nurse could say anything. "I woke up, and he was in my lap. Honest."

"He would have been too weak and in too much pain to do that on his own," said the nurse.

"That's what I thought, but I swear to you he came over here on his own. I woke up because my left arm was feeling numb. I woke up and found him lying here in my lap."

"She told me the same thing," blurted Tony, "when I asked her why she removed him from the bed."

As the nurse was explaining how unlikely Rose's story was, Rose and Tony tried to suppress their smiles. They saw that Trey had woke up again. They watched him unhook the monitor and climb down from the bed. He slowly walked over to Rose, right past the nurse, and climbed up into her lap. He curled himself up into a ball and closed his eyes. Tony and Rose looked at the nurse as if to say I told you so.

"I don't believe what I'm seeing," said the nurse. "Even if he is in no pain, which he should be, he should be far too weak to be moving around so effortlessly. This is amazing!" said the nurse as she felt Trey's forehead once more. "Dr. Rosen will want to know about this," she exclaimed as she almost ran out of the room.

Tony and Rose watched the nurse as she left, looked at each other, and began to laugh. Tony got up, walked over to the light switch, turned it off, and then returned to his recliner. Rose lay back with Trey in her lap and pulled the blanket over both of them. She knew deep in her heart that Trey would be okay. Tony reached over and held her hand, and without knowing what the other was doing, they both gave God the glory and said a prayer of thanks in their mind.

Twenty minutes later Dr. Rosen and the nurse both came through the door. Again, the nurse turned on the light. Hurriedly, they walked over to Rose. Without removing Trey from his mother's lap, Dr. Rosen checked him for a fever and took his pulse. He told them that the nurse had told him everything, and he wanted to conduct more tests. He apologized for having to awaken Trey and run the tests at such an unconventional hour, but he convinced them of how important it was. Actually, the urgency was all Dr. Rosen's curiosity. The testing could have waited, but he did not tell that to Rose or Tony.

Dr. Rosen lifted Trey from his mother's lap and headed for the door, with the nurse right behind him. As Rose and Tony began to follow them out, Rose decided to text her parents to tell them the good news. When she removed her cell phone from her purse, she became startled because her phone started ringing. In fact, all four of their cell phones started ringing simultaneously. When they looked at their phones, it was exactly 11:25 p.m. Dr. Rosen and the nurse ignored their ringing phones and hurried out of the room.

CHAPTER 13

THE CHALLENGE

At that precise moment over at the W.O.R.D. conference, the stage shook as if it were in the middle of an earthquake. Atulya Kumar held on to the podium for dear life as they both fell over. The four Hindus behind him fell out of their chairs. They lay flat on their stomach trying to wait it out. The audience looked on but did not know what to think. They were perfectly fine and had not been affected by the rumbling. The shaking of the stage lasted only about five minutes, but it seemed to go on much longer. The five people on the stage stayed on the floor for another thirty seconds after the shaking stopped. They wanted to be sure it was over. As they slowly got up, a couple of stagehands came out to reassemble the stage. They found that only the podium and the chairs had to be reset. The scenery held up just fine. There was a loud mumbling in the audience that permeated the entire auditorium. Atulya Kumar gathered himself and stepped back up to the podium. He held his throat and tested his voice to see if it had returned. It had.

"It seems that the foundation of this stage is not as sturdy as it should be. As I was saying, the Hindu way of life has been copied for centuries. There is one thing that has been copied more than any other and that is the attempt to unite the outer self with the inner spirit. This can be done with the proper training, and when mastered, you can experience god in your inner spirit. I am sure that all of you have heard of this training, and a great number of you have probably tried it. The process of uniting the outer self with the inner spirit is called yoga. Many of you are undercover Hindus."

A low burst of laughter came from the crowd, but most of the audience was still thinking about the quake-like tremors. They were still a bit uneasy and half of them believed that the stage had not been properly secured. The other half was a bit more pessimistic and thought that something more sinister was the reason for the tremors.

"There is yet another theory of Hinduism that all of you have heard of and believe in, without knowing its origin. You speak of it daily without realizing that you are embracing Hindu philosophy. I am speaking of the moral law of cause and effect, in which we all believe that every action, good or bad, has consequences. The Hindu term for this is Karma. I can tell by the look on your faces that you did not know that the belief in Karma is an original Hindu philosophy."

"While you digest that the beliefs of yoga and Karma have their origin in Hinduism, let me tell you one more very important fact that most religions, especially Christianity, copied from the Hindus. You see the Hindus have a word for the ultimate goal of life. That word is Moksha. The ultimate goal of life is to obtain Moksha, which is an eternal union with God, free from worldly desires, sorrow, and pain and living in Loka. Loka is another Hindu term, but most of you refer to it as heaven. So, whether you realize it or not, all of you Christians, Catholics, Methodists, Presbyterians, or whatever you call yourself, already practice the Hindu way of life. You should seriously think about converting to Hinduism. You already enjoy the part of our faith that you are familiar with. Why not immerse yourselves into our faith completely and get away from the copycat religions. The only thing separating Christianity from Hinduism is the belief in Jesus Christ as the Messiah. He is nothing but an old wives' tale."

At that exact moment, the tremors returned to the stage. This time they were much more violent and more damaging. Everything on the stage that wasn't on the floor was thrown to the floor, including the background scenery. The Hindu representatives were tossed around like dolls as they fought for their lives. The audience was paralyzed with uncertainty. They didn't know what to do. The rest of the venue was unaffected, but the stage seemed to be possessed.

A couple of stagehands and a few brave members of the audience tried to help. They went to the stage and tried to grab the Hindus. This was difficult because when the rumbling stage struck their body it was very painful. A third stagehand came out with a rope and threw one end of it on the stage while holding on to the other end. One by one they were able to pull the Hindus from the stage. One of the Hindus was able to roll off the stage on his own. The rumbling stopped when the last person was pulled from the stage. No one could believe what they had just witnessed. It was as if the stage were purposely trying to remove the people from it.

The entire audience erupted into conversation as the stagehands inspected the stage. Everyone had an idea of what had just happened, and most of them came to the same conclusion. They thought that the building was not stable. The stage was the only thing being affected at the moment, but many of them believed that the entire building would soon come down on top of them. A couple of dozen people left the building complaining and demanding their money back.

Gwen had her own theory, and she was eager to tell it to John. She had noticed that the stage started to shake violently each time the Hindu representative spoke negatively about Christianity or Jesus. Of course, she didn't believe the negative jabs the guy was getting in, but she did find the information interesting. She knew that this kind of talk was very dangerous for those Christians who were young in the faith, who were on the fence and not sure what to believe. She knew it was dangerous also for those whose faith had been shaken due to personal circumstances. Gwen swore that she felt the presence of God in the building. Little did she know that John had come to some of the same conclusions.

"This is a little strange," whispered Gwen as she turned to talk to John. "You're not going to leave too, are you?"

"No, no," said John, "but I agree that it is weird for the stage to be shaking so violently when nothing else in the building is affected."

"It happened not once but twice. Did you notice what was going on when the stage started shaking so violently?"

"You mean right after the guy started criticizing Christ?" asked John.

"You noticed that huh? Don't tell me you think that's a coincidence."

"Good question," said John. "That's exactly what I'm trying to determine. However, I do sense some type of electricity in the atmosphere. I can't put my finger on it, but I have a bit of an uneasy feeling."

"That's the Holy Spirit in the building," said Gwen.

John didn't respond. He didn't deny it, but he wasn't ready just yet to let Gwen know that he agreed with her. His focus remained on the men still checking out the stage. They looked over every inch of it. Gwen didn't push John for a reply. He had been preoccupied the entire day, and she could tell that he was struggling with something. She prayed that he was preoccupied about his faith, the faith he used to have, the faith his grandmother had. Until today it had been a long time since John did not reply with a negative response when she mentioned something about God, or Christ, or faith. His inclination not to reply was better than a negative one, and she accepted that as progress. The stagehands and maintenance crew checked the stage for thirty minutes, and it appeared as if they were about finished. They reconstructed the stage and scenery to look as it had before that last violent tremor. Once again Reed Pierce approached the microphone on the corner of the stage, as a few people continued to leave.

"Ladies and gentlemen, I apologize for the delay, but we have to make sure that the stage is safe. Maintenance found no problems anywhere. Not only have they examined the stage area thoroughly, but they have also looked over the entire auditorium, upstairs and downstairs. Everything seems to be in order. We have no idea what caused those tremors, but our guests are willing to demonstrate their faith in their god by continuing with the program. Next up is the nation of Islam. Islam is the second-largest religion in the world with over 1.8 billion followers. Without further delay, I present to you the Nation of Islam."

The Islam representatives came to the stage and immediately dropped to their hands and knees. They formed a circle with each one placing their arms on the floor from their elbow to the tips of their fingers, with their palms face down on the floor. They prayed in this position for three minutes before rising. Like the other religions that had appeared before them, the representatives of the Nation of Islam all took a seat except the speaker, who walked to the podium.

"Hello, ladies and gentlemen, my name is Khalid Abdul-Aalee, which means eternal servant of the most-high. As Reed Pierce said, the Nation of Islam has the second-largest following in the world, but we are steadily closing in on the Christians. Our faith was founded by Muhammad, and as you know, our followers are referred to as Muslims. Muhammad is often referred to as the last prophet of God. He was also known as the messenger of Allah because Muhammad created the Quran. The Quran is the word of God given to Muhamad by the archangel Gabriel, to bring the will of God to the world. The Quran is our religious text, which has one hundred and fourteen chapters."

"The Muslim faith is similar to Christianity in a lot of ways, but it is different in one major way. Like the Christians, we believe there is only one God, and he is the creator of everything by simply speaking it into existence. However, Muslims reject the Christian belief of the Trinity. Muslims believe that Jesus was a prophet, not the son of God. Therefore, we do not believe in his death and resurrection."

"Enough," rang out a strong voice that echoed through the building and shattered the silence. "I have heard enough. This is blasphemy."

A loud sound, similar to a clap of thunder, rocked the stage violently for ten seconds. Everyone in the auditorium jumped, and half of them started screaming. Everything on the stage fell to the floor, including the Muslims. The podium exploded, but the shards of wood did not propel very far. It was a controlled explosion as if the podium were inside of an invisible container of some sort. The shards were propelled only about three feet in every direction and then fell to the floor.

Everyone looked around trying to identify the origin of the voice, but it was impossible to locate because it filled the entire auditorium and seemed to originate from the air itself. The audience had seen enough, and people started to make their way to the exits. The voice uttered a simple command, "Go back to your seat!"

Everyone stopped in their tracks, turned around, and returned to their seat. They did not understand why they were obeying the voice, but they felt helpless to resist. They were scared, but they turned their attention back to the Muslims, who were rolling around on the stage. They were more stunned than hurt as they checked themselves for injuries. As the Muslims made it to their feet, the audience noticed two bright red lights coming down the center aisle. As the red lights got closer, they recognized that the lights were being held by a man. No, the red lights were the hands of a man. His hands were not just bright red, they looked to be covered with blood and pulsating with power.

John and Gwen sat up in their seats. They both recognized him. Gwen remembered him from the newscast, and John would never forget the conversation he had had with Simon the night before.

"That's the guy from the news," said Gwen.

"That's him," said John simultaneously.

"Him who?" asked Gwen as she turned to face John. "How do you know him?"

"That's what I was about to ask you. How do you know him?"

"I saw him on the late news a few nights ago. Where have you seen him?"

"I spoke with him last night when I was walking home. He came to me out of the shadows. He startled me at first."

"What did he want?"

"It's a long story."

"The sooner you start, the sooner you'll finish."

"His name is Simon, and he knew all about me. He knew things about me that even I had forgotten. I thought he was some kind of con at first, but I've been having second thoughts. He reminded me about how my faith used to be much stronger, and about how I was closer to God years ago. I did not want to tell you about it right away because I knew what you would say. I needed to work some things out in my mind first."

"So that's why you have been acting so different today."

"He told me that Trey's healing depends on my faith."

"Tonight, is a night that some of you will never forget," said Simon, "and the rest of you will wish you could forget. Only a select few of you will remember me, but all of you will remember the power of Jesus, which will be on display tonight. My identity is unimportant, but I will have very little sympathy for anyone who denies the identity and the power of Jesus after tonight. Some of you have been chosen to spread the gospel through your God-given talents. You will encounter some difficult moments but remember that Jesus is working through you. You are loved and highly favored. Never forget that, no matter what else you may face in your life."

All eyes turned to Simon, who had now reached the stage. John and Gwen, as was everyone in the audience, were in awe of this tall, muscular Black man who looked like a professional athlete. Simon's physical physique was impressive and created a lot of chatter, but his red hands glowing with power was the main subject of everyone's conversation. Gwen felt a connection with him, although she had never met him before. John, too, felt a connection with him but for a different reason. They both felt the presence of the Holy Spirit. While

Gwen felt relaxed and at ease, John felt very uncomfortable and guilty.

"I have heard enough of this blasphemy," continued Simon. "For over two hours, I have listened to each group deny Christ as Lord. If they acknowledged him at all, they called him a mere man. Some of you called Him a prophet, and some of you consider Him a fairy tale."

Simon paused for a minute as he noticed police officers and plain-clothed policemen approaching him slowly from all sides.

"Stop," Simon commanded. "I command all law enforcement to go to the top level and stay there until I release you. Put your weapons away and be silent. Everyone else stay in your seat."

The officers did as Simon commanded. They all went back up to the top of the auditorium. A couple of dozen law enforcement personnel, who were strategically mixed in with the audience, stood up, made their way through the aisles, and went to the top of the auditorium.

"As I was saying," continued Simon, "some of you equate Christ to an old wife's tale. You don't believe in his resurrection, and for that, your souls are lost and you will burn forever. Before this night is over, you will know the power of Christ. I am a servant of the Messiah, and He has given me the authority on this night to remind those of you who already know Him, to convince those of you who do not believe in Him and to warn those of you who blaspheme His name that He is alive and has all power in his hands. Except for the Christians, I want the speaker of each faith to come to the stage now."

Each religious leader slowly walked onto the stage. They tried to resist Simon's command, but they couldn't. The Muslim spokesman was the first one on the stage because he was the closest. One by one each one arrived. They formed a line across the stage facing the audience. Simon snapped the fingers of his right hand, and all the scenery, microphones, chairs, and what was left of the podium instantly disappeared. The audience gasped loudly. John was feeling humble and insignificant. Gwen was totally immersed in what was happening on the stage. Simon continued, as he could be heard clearly throughout the auditorium without the use of a microphone.

"Each of you has promoted your faith while criticizing the Christians. Yet, while promoting your faith, you compared it to Christianity. I think you did this because you know that Christianity is the standard that every other faith is trying to reach. You claim that Christianity copied your philosophy, but it's just the opposite. The Hindus claim to be the oldest faith on the planet, but Christianity can be traced back to the very creation of the earth itself. You date Christ from His earthly birth, but Christ was here in the beginning."

"I challenge each of you to show me what your god can do. Then I will show you what my God can do."

"Oh my God," said Gwen under her breath! "This is the bible coming to life."

"It does remind me of Elijah challenging the prophets of Baal in the eighteenth chapter of First Kings," said John

"That's exactly what it is," said Gwen. "This is unbelievable."

"Do any of you have anything to say?" asked Simon. "This is your opportunity to back up your boasting by showing the people how powerful your god is. Tell your gods to strike me down because I challenge them in the name of Jesus Christ."

None of the religious leaders said a word. They looked at each other and at Simon and wondered how they had gotten into this predicament.

"Your faith seems to have left you," said Simon. Let me help you out. Look up at the screens hanging above you."

Each person on stage and the entire audience looked up. The screens no longer showed what was happening on stage. They were showing the tsunami hitting the coast of Japan. Not only were the people in the audience witnessing the devastation in real-time, but everyone around the world who was tuned in to the W.O.R.D. was seeing it as well. Again, a loud gasp permeated through the audience, as they watched what appeared to be total devastation. A broadcaster could be heard in a language that everyone understood, describing the catastrophe that was taking place. The broadcaster explained that the city of Honshu was steadily being ripped apart by the earthquake, while the giant waves were destroying what the earthquake didn't.

"Call on your gods!" demanded Simon. "Ask him to help those people. You'd better hurry," said Simon sarcastically, "it doesn't look as if they have much time. You call on your god, and then I will call on mine. We will see whose god is really God!"

The leaders of the various religions began to pray. Most of them dropped to their knees, but a few continued to stand. A few of them prayed out loud, but most prayed silently. The ones who were standing began to chant in their native language, as they clasped their hands together and lifted their heads upward. Simon continued to mock them.

"This all seems a bit chaotic to me," mocked Simon. "I hope you're not confusing your gods. Hey guys, those people can't tread water much longer. A lot of them have already been swallowed by the waves. Pray harder!" Simon commanded.

The religious leaders prayed harder. They began to sweat profusely. A few had tears streaming down their face. The tsunami had totally engulfed the beach, and the water started to invade the streets of the city. Every vehicle that stood in its path was soon swept away by the giant waves, along with street signs and telephone poles. Buildings could be seen shaking and crumbling before the waves swallowed them. The audience screamed in horror, and some cried as they witnessed people being swept away by the water.

"Enough!" shouted Simon. "This wailing and blubbering is not only blasphemy but it's hurting my ears. Stand up and witness the power of my God. Witness the power of Jesus Christ, whom you so cold-heartedly and eagerly tried to discredit. When this night is over, I pray that the Lord will have mercy on your souls."

Simon looked up at one of the screens with a scowl on his face, and the audience became silent. They had witnessed some of his power and wondered what was coming next. You could hear the proverbial pin drop. The people on stage looked back and forth from one another to the screen. Some members of the audience looked as if they were watching a tennis match. They would look at Simon, look at the screen, then look at Simon, then look back at the screen. Simon's hands were visibly pulsating with power, and they were glowing brighter. He pointed at the screen and shouted two words: "Be still!" Instantly the buildings ceased shaking and stopped crumbling. The earthquake under the ocean relaxed. The giant waves still crashed the city, but the buildings were holding together. Faces popped up in the windows of the buildings that were still standing. They could be seen crying and hugging each other as satellite cameras zoomed in. The broadcaster tried to explain what had just happened. He mentioned that he had just gotten a report from the Japan Meteorological Agency, announcing that all seismic activity had ceased. They were not getting any readings of an earthquake. Everyone's eyes were on Simon as he continued to point to the screen.

Simon spoke once again. "Retreat!" he shouted. The giant waves stopped rushing through the city. The water stayed perfectly still for about twenty seconds, then started to flow back to the ocean. Like the parting of the Red Sea, the ground was dry when the water retreated. The audience had mixed emotions. Some cheered and clapped as if they were watching a movie. Others appeared nervous and scared, but those who were in the Spirit were in awe. They knew they were witnessing the power of God and felt very humble, yet grateful. As the water retreated to the ocean, extreme grief entered the hearts of everyone who was watching. Though not one fish or sea-dwelling creature could be seen, the retreating water revealed a gruesome scene. The streets looked like a graveyard of unburied bodies. Arms and legs could be seen protruding from the rubble of fallen buildings.

This was more than some could bear. Some tried to leave their seats but couldn't. They were still under Simon's command to stay in their seat. A few people turned their heads and put their hands over their mouths to keep from vomiting. Cries of sorrow could be heard throughout the audience. Simon stayed focused as the last drops of water withdrew back into the ocean. The height of the water dropped to its normal level, and the sand on the beach could once again be seen.

Again, Simon spoke to the screen. "As you were!" he commanded. Like a film being run in reverse, the demolished buildings start to stand back up, in perfect condition. Though the dead bodies were still lying in the streets, this miraculous scene commanded the attention of everyone. Slowly, one by one, each building that had crumbled started to stand back up. John and Gwen held hands as they witnessed the power of God. They were not scared. They were thrilled beyond belief. After thirty minutes every building that had fallen was back in place. Even the telephone poles stood back up, and the electrical lines reconnected.

"What about the people?" someone shouted. "Can you revive the people?"

"Is there anything too hard for God?" Simon asked.

Simon pointed to the screen. "Breathe," he commanded.

Nothing happened for two minutes as every eye was glued to the screens. Suddenly a low murmur spread through the audience. The low murmur soon turned into shouts of joy and excitement. As the broadcaster explained what was happening, the cameras zoomed in. The people were coming back to life. You could see the inhaling and exhaling motions from the chests of hundreds of people who had been injured in the devastation. After a few more minutes, the victims of the tsunami began to spew the ocean water from their lungs. They opened their eyes, sat up, and looked around. The audience broke into a loud cheer, with some laughter, as they witnessed small children stand up and run around as their parents chased after them. Everything returned to the way it was before the tsunami. People, who moments ago were buried under tons of rubble from the demolished buildings, were now staring out of the windows of those same buildings. The audience continued to clap and cheer.

"As I asked earlier, is there anything too hard for God?" Simon repeated. He turned to the religious leaders on stage. "All of you need to repent. You should be on your knees praying right now, begging the Lord for forgiveness. Get out of here," Simon ordered. "Go back to where you came from and pray that you make it back safely."

One by one the religious leaders left as Simon commanded. When they had all left the stage, they were joined by their companions. They did not exit through the stage curtains as they had entered. They left from the front of the stage and walked up the center aisle. The audience did not harass or heckle them as they passed by. They simply watched them leave in disgrace without saying a word.

"If you are wise, you will never forget what you have witnessed here tonight. Even more important than what you witnessed, is the power behind it. That is not my power. I have no power. That is the power of Jesus. I am but a messenger of hope, who was sent to remind you that Jesus is real and has all power in his hands." Simon held both of his hands out in front of him. "The next time you hear the phrase there is power in the blood, you will swear by it. As I said earlier, only a select few of you will remember me because God will get the glory, not I."

"Before I leave, Jesus has a message for each one of you. It's a message meant just for you and your circumstances. The time is exactly 11:15 p.m. At exactly 11:25 p.m., the cell phone of every person in the world will ring, according to the ring tone they have chosen. If you own a cell phone, it will ring until you answer it. If your ringer is turned off, if your phone is on vibrate, or even if your phone is completely turned off, it will still ring. Though you will hear your ring tone, your message will be in the form of a text. Every message will be written in the language you understand best, will end with "I love you," and will be signed by the Lamb of God."

Simon jumped from the stage to the floor. He headed toward the center aisle and left the same way he entered. When he reached the top, he quickly left the building and then released everyone from his power. All law enforcement officers quickly raced toward the exits, but

Simon was nowhere to be found. He was right across the street hiding in the shadows, watching the officers running both ways up and down the street. At least a dozen of them had looked directly at him, but they could not see him. Lieutenant Perkins stood at the edge of the curb and looked in the general location in which Simon was standing. He stood there for about a minute and stared into the darkness. He could not see Simon, but it was as if he had sensed something. Perkins turned to his left and walked down the street as the audience began leaving the building. Suddenly, his cell phone began to ring.

CHAPTER 14

PRAYER WORKS

Like everyone else, John and Gwen hurried to leave the building. John held Gwen's hand firmly as they made their way through the crowd. Gwen was feeling a little emotional. The event tonight surpassed her wildest dreams, and John's tenderness and attentiveness touched her. She felt young and in love all over again. If her grandson was not in the hospital, Gwen would swear that she was dreaming.

John was in awe and wasn't quite sure how to decipher the last twenty-four hours. His conversation with Simon the night before started out guarded and unbelievable, and then it became incriminating and humbling. Simon had reminded him not only of how blessed he was but also of how selfish he had been. When he thought about that conversation and realized that Simon was telling the truth, he felt so guilty.

He made up his mind that not only would he be a better husband, but he would strive to be a better Christian. Simon had touched him in a way in which no one else had ever done, except his grandmother. It made him feel awful when he thought about how much his grandmother had sacrificed for him. Now, less than twenty-four hours later, to live through what he had just witnessed was a very humbling experience. He didn't have the words to explain how he was feeling. John rationalized that Simon was a living miracle sent from God to remind people like him that God is real and is still in control.

John was moving on instinct at this point as he maneuvered his way through the crowd. He was preoccupied with everything that had happened and he was trying to make sense of it all. He was trying to figure out why Simon had spoken face-to-face to him specifically. Of all the people on the planet, why did Simon reach out to him? He knew that others had lost a child or grandchild and were hurting. Why did Simon speak to him right before he showed the world the power of God? He was not sure how he felt about that. He kept playing this over and over in his mind as he and Gwen approached the exit.

A few yards before they reached the exit, they heard a noise that spread through the entire auditorium. It was the unmistakable sound of the standard cell phone ringing, though some unique and commercial ring tones played as well. Regardless of the tone, the crowd stopped in their tracks and looked for their phone. John and Gwen did likewise. Then they all realized that it was exactly 11:25, and Simon's words had become reality. The crowd became instantly silent as they glanced at their phones and then at one another.

As Simon had proclaimed, each person had received a unique text message from Jesus. Some people cried, some just smiled, and a few let out a small outburst of anger. Some people immediately fell to their knees, while others clasped their hands together in prayer. The Lamb of God had spoken to each one of them.

John and Gwen were just as surprised as everyone else. They were filled with emotion as they read their texts. John tried to hurry and wipe the tears from his eyes, but no one was judging anyone at that moment. They were both speechless, and John pulled his wife to him and gave her a big hug. They exchanged phones to read each other's message.

"Gwen, you have truly been a blessing to Me. You are highly favored, and your faith has been rewarded. I love you, the Lamb of God."

"John, I have always been with you. You can talk to Me anytime. I would love to hear from you. I love you, the Lamb of God."

As John and Gwen read each other's message, they couldn't help but cry. They returned each other's phone, wiped their eyes, and held hands as they walked toward the exit. When they got outside, they crossed the street and returned to the stop where the shuttle bus had let them off. A group of people was already there, and no one was saying anything. They didn't have to wait long before their bus pulled up. Everyone boarded the bus, took a seat, and became lost in thought. John and Gwen continued to hold hands as they rode quietly in the night.

Though still feeling a little shell-shocked, John and Gwen both felt as if a weight had been lifted from their shoulders. John realized that life was really simple if you followed Jesus. Yes, there would be difficult times, but Jesus promised to never leave or forsake us. We just have to follow him, trust him, and believe him. That's what faith is—trusting and believing in God without knowing when, where, or how. John had stayed away for so long, but now he felt as if he were back on the right path. The ride back to their car seemed much shorter than the one to the venue. Before they knew it, they were at their stop.

John and Gwen exited the bus and headed in the general direction of their car. Gwen was on cloud nine and had already decided that she would never erase that text. She was also thinking about going somewhere to have it printed and then framing it. She got her phone out so that she could read the text again. As she opened her phone, she saw a text from her daughter. She read it and started crying once again. John was clueless as to what was going on until he heard her sniffling. He turned to her and began to wipe her tears away.

"What's wrong?" he asked. "This has been a wonderful night. Why are you crying?"

"Read this text from Rose," said Gwen as she handed him her phone.

"This is good news," said John after he finished reading the text. "This is really good news. Those are tears of joy. I thought they were tears of sadness."

"No," said Gwen, "they are tears of joy. I am not sure how much more good news I can take tonight. Twenty-four hours ago, it seemed as if you were losing hope, and I must admit that my faith was starting to wane too. Tonight, all is right with the world. It's as if we just woke up from a bad dream and discovered that everything is fine."

"That is exactly what happened," agreed John. "That's an excellent way to put it. Rose said that Trey's procedure went very well and that he was doing much better than the doctor had expected. She said that the doctor is running more tests on Trey. He must be doing well to run tests at this time of night. Let's go by the hospital and see him."

"Don't you think that visiting hours have been over with for a while? We won't be able to see him at this hour."

"Sure, we will," said John. "The staff knows the medical issues we have had with Trey and with Junior before him. They will be glad to give us good news for a change."

"Maybe, you're right," said Gwen. "Let's give it a try.

After a few minutes, John and Gwen had reached their car. It took them a while to leave their parking area due to the heavy traffic. The slow traffic did not upset them because they knew it would be bumper to bumper for a while. After the night they had just experienced, it would take a lot to bring them down. Besides knowing that Trey was doing well made all the difference in the world. The wait would make their arrival that much better.

Traffic let up a little, and they started to move a bit faster. Gwen silently praised and thanked God for Trey's positive medical report. She had been asking for an improvement in Trey's health since his birth. Since Junior had died of amyloidosis, Trey's parents had him tested soon after his birth to see if he had inherited that same dreadful condition. The entire family was heartbroken when the tests came back positive. Now, Gwen was sure that her prayers had been answered. She could feel it. She believed it. She claimed it.

Gwen was enjoying the slow ride as she was able to people watch a little more. She noticed all the out-of-town license plates and tried to count how many different states she saw. She kept losing count because her thoughts would go back to the hospital with Trey. Suddenly she thought about something. She wondered if Trey's improvement had anything to do with the experiments of Junior's blood being mixed with Dr. Richards's blood. Even though she gave God the credit, God could have worked through Dr. Richards. Dr. Rosen had given Trey a new treatment that he had wanted to try. She had never told John about the research using Junior's blood. She thought that this was the perfect time to tell him.

"I have something to tell you, John. I hope you don't get angry."

"I'm not sure how I should respond to that," answered John. "We have had such a wonderful evening that I don't think anything can spoil it. Though, from the sound of your voice, I am not so sure. However, I will try my best to keep a level head. What's bothering you, baby?"

"Do you remember the night that Junior died?"

"Of course, I do. I will never forget it."

"Do you remember how upset you were and how you decided to walk home after the doctors told us that Junior had passed away?"

"Yes, that was the longest night of my life. Where are you going with this?"

"Soon after you left, an ambulance brought a young boy to the hospital. He had been in an automobile accident. His father was driving and suffered a massive heart attack and died. They were on their way to the hospital to pick up his mother who worked there."

"Was the boy okay?"

"Yes, he was fine. He just had a scratch on his forehead. John, that boy's father was a pastor."

"Honey, I feel for the boy's loss, but why would that news upset me?"

"I haven't come to the upsetting part yet."

John was starting to feel a little anxious and a little guilty. He knew that the boy Gwen was telling him about was the same child he stopped to help, and he had not told her about it. He couldn't have done anything for the boy's father, but he did try to console the child, and he called the hospital and reported the accident. He was curious as to where Gwen was going with this.

"OK, honey, go on," said John.

"It turns out that boy's blood was a perfect match to Junior's. His name is Kevin Richards. The doctor told me back then that if Kevin had arrived at the hospital an hour earlier, there was a slight possibility that a blood transfusion from him to Junior could have helped Junior. He said that it was a long shot, but it definitely was the best scenario at the time.

"After all these years, why are you telling me this now?" asked John.

"Honey, that's not the upsetting part. But it appears that you are already upset, and I haven't finished telling you what I need to say."

"Baby, I am not upset. I am just curious why this has been such a big secret all these years."

"John, what I haven't told you all these years is that I approved for the doctors to use Junior's blood for medical research so that they could try and find a cure for amyloidosis. They believed that using Junior's blood, along with that child's blood, could help to find a cure for this dreadful disease."

John was silent for a few moments. He was not angry, but he wondered why his wife thought he would be. Apparently, his selfish behavior over the years had influenced her more than he knew, and he started to feel even more guilty. He knew he had to come clean and tell his wife the part he played that night regarding the young boy. He tried to appear calm, which he was.

"So after over twenty years of research how much progress has been made?"

"I am not sure exactly, but I was told that they have made significant progress. In fact, I am pretty sure that the treatment Trey was given earlier today involved that research."

"Wow!" exclaimed John, "You mean that it's possible, in an ironic sort of way, that Junior is helping to cure his nephew?"

"I never thought of it that way," said Gwen, "but I firmly believe that to be true. Here's another ironic fact about this situation. That young boy is now Dr. Richards, who is an intern at that same hospital."

"This is great news. This is really great news."

"I'm so glad that you're not upset. You're right, honey; I should have told you about this a long time ago."

"Yes, you should have, but I can't be upset with you. There's a part to this story that I have never told you about, so I am just as guilty."

"What are you talking about?"

"Gwen, when I left the hospital on the night that Junior died, I was so upset that I couldn't see straight. I was angry with the world and wanted everyone to hurt as badly as I was hurting. Before I knew it, a car sped right past me and crashed into a light pole. The driver looked pretty banged up, but I kept walking."

"John, you didn't! You didn't try to help…? Wait a minute. Are you telling me the accident you saw that night was the one involving the boy I just told you about?"

"Yes, that's exactly what I'm telling you."

"You were hurting so bad that you couldn't help that child and his father?"

"Let me finish, baby. I did keep walking at first, but I went back to see if whoever was in the car was okay. As I said, the driver was pretty banged up, and I thought that he was gone. I was about to go find a phone to call it in when I heard some noise coming from the back seat. That's when I saw a cute, green-eyed child crying. I tried to calm him down. He had a small cut on his forehead, but it wasn't a serious injury. I pulled out my handkerchief, pressed it against his forehead, and told him to hold it there. He was still whining a little, so I gave him the cross necklace that my grandmother had given to me."

"John, you loved that necklace. I have wondered what happened to it. I thought that you just stopped wearing it because you were mad at God."

"Well, that I can't deny. I was mad at God. That cross seemed to calm him down, and I wasn't sure I wanted it anymore. However, I then left and found a phone and called the hospital."

"You're the one who called the hospital about that accident?"

"Yes, I called the hospital and told them about an accident that was practically right outside their door. I told them about the child and the driver. I told them that the child was okay, but the driver was seriously hurt. I gave the hospital the name of the street, and they said they were on their way."

"John, I'm proud of you. That's the man I married. I knew you were hurting really bad, but I couldn't imagine you leaving without trying to do something to help."

"That night was a real test for me. I shiver now when I think about it. To even think that I could be so cold and uncaring scares me. I know that my attitude over the last twenty years has been terrible, and I don't know how you put up with me. I have been in a twenty-year pity party, and it's way past time I come out of it. Gwen, I apologize for everything I have put you through and for being so selfish in only thinking of myself."

"No need to apologize. I understand. I have had my moments too. After Junior died, I was so protective of Rose that I almost alienated her."

"We almost alienated her," corrected John. "I was right there with you. I'm glad we realized what we were doing before it was too late."

"I wonder if Dr. Richards still has that cross. I know it meant the world to you."

"I just hope it meant something to the young boy who had just lost his father. I am glad I gave it to him if it helped. If it meant half as much to him as it meant to me, it was worth it."

John turned onto the street leading to the hospital. He circled around past the emergency room entrance and went into the parking garage. He had to drive through a couple of levels of the garage until he found a parking spot. John and Gwen entered the building, took the elevator to the seventh floor, walked down the hall, and turned the corner to get to Trey's room. When they entered the room, they were a bit surprised to find it empty.

"Where is everybody?" asked Gwen with concern that was evident in her voice.

"I am sure everything is okay," said John. "Let's go to the nurse's station and find out where everyone is."

As they left the room, Gwen grabbed John's hand. The nurse's station wasn't far, but they were not in a hurry. The lone nurse at the station was on the phone, and they had to wait a few minutes for her to finish her conversation.

"Hello, how may I help you?" asked the nurse. "I hope you're not here to see a patient because visiting hours ended at 8:00 p.m."

"We understand that," said John, "but our daughter called us about forty-five minutes ago and told us that our grandson was about to undergo more testing. We were hoping that it would be alright if we came up."

"That's unusual," said the nurse, "testing is never done at this time of night. Are you sure the testing wasn't scheduled for tomorrow morning?"

"We're sure," said John. "It seems that our grandson is doing better than expected, and Dr. Rosen wanted to run some tests right away."

"I did see Dr. Rosen come through here about an hour ago. He is never at the hospital this late unless it is a true emergency. What is your grandson's name?

"His name is Trey, Trey Thompson," said John.

"Ok, let me take a look. I do see a note here in the computer for a Trey Thompson. It appears that you are correct. He is undergoing some testing down on the fifth floor. It looks as if the testing is finished, and they're wrapping up down there. Why don't you two go to his room and wait for him there? They should be back up in a few minutes."

"Thank you," said John. "We will do that."

"Yes, thank you," said Gwen.

"You are welcome," said the nurse.

John and Gwen headed back toward Trey's room. Gwen was a little more at ease. The nurse was very professional, and she showed no signs of anything being wrong. Gwen knew that Rose's message was a positive one, but she was still a bit guarded. She didn't want to get her hopes up too high. When they reached the room, they headed toward the recliners that Tony and Rose had been sleeping in. They pushed the blankets to one side and made themselves comfortable.

"A penny for your thoughts?" asked Gwen.

"I'm too ashamed to share them," said John.

"Baby, as much as we have been through, we should be able to talk about anything."

"You're absolutely right. I just feel so bad about all the time I have wasted being angry. Starting at this very moment, I am going to try to focus on the positive things in my life. I love Trey to death, and I pray that he can beat this amyloidosis disease. If he doesn't, I will be heartbroken, but in the meantime, I will make sure to cherish every moment we have with him."

"I'm proud of you, John. The first step in thinking positive is to remove the negative, such as doubt. Don't use words like if and maybe. You have to claim that Trey will be healed and believe it in your heart. Then trust God to reward your faith."

Before John could respond, the door opened. Tony and Rose walked in. Tony was carrying Trey, who was asleep. John and Gwen stood up simultaneously as Tony placed Trey in the bed and pulled the cover over him. When he finished, Gwen and John exchanged hugs with Tony and Rose. Gwen jumped right in with the questions. She couldn't hold her composure any longer.

"How is my baby," asked Gwen? "Is he going to be okay? Why are they running tests on him now? Why does he have a big bandage on his arm?"

"Calm down, Mom, calm down," said Tony. "Trey is fine. As a matter of fact, he is better than fine."

"He is better than fine? What does that mean?" asked Gwen.

"Well," said Rose, "the doctors drew more blood from Trey. He cried when they stuck him, but he's fine now. Earlier this evening, I woke up and found Trey in my lap. I was still half asleep, and I thought we were at home, so I was going to take him back to his bed. Then I realized that we were still here at the hospital. When Trey left his bed to come to me, he pulled the heart monitor off himself, which alerted the nursing station that he was flat lining. The nurse rushed in here and went straight to his bed. Of course, he wasn't there. She looked around the room and saw him in my lap. Well, she marched over to my recliner, took Trey from me, placed him back in bed, and reconnected the heart monitor. Then she came back over to scold me for taking him from his bed. I tried to explain that he came over here on his own, but she refused to believe it."

"This is the funny part," interrupted Tony. "While the nurse was scolding Rose and telling her how weak he was and how he would sleep through the night, Trey walked right past her and climbed back into Rose's lap. The nurse's eyes almost popped out of her head."

"Apparently my grandson isn't as weak as they think," boasted John.

"The nurse called Dr. Rosen right away," continued Rose. The next thing we know Dr. Rosen bursts through the door and grabs Trey. He left mumbling something about conducting more tests on him. That's when I sent you a quick text while we followed the doctor to the fifth floor."

"Your text said something about Trey doing really well," said John. "What is that about?"

"That's what we have been trying to tell you," said Rose.

"According to the nurse and the doctor, Trey should have been in a lot of pain and should have been pretty weak. On top of that, they thought he had enough pain killer in him to make him sleep through the night. You see, Trey is acting like any normal little boy at bedtime. He was feeling fine and was showing no ill effects from the procedure he had just gone through."

"Are you saying what I think you're saying?" asked John.

"Yes," answered Rose with tears flowing down her cheeks. "It's a miracle. The tests the doctors just ran showed no signs of amyloidosis."

"Praise God!" exclaimed Gwen.

"They want to keep Trey here at least another twenty-four hours," said Tony. "They want to make sure the test results are not false. If his progress continues tomorrow, he will be released Monday morning.

"No trace of the disease is showing?" asked John with enthusiasm.

"Not in the preliminary test," said Tony. "The results of the main test won't be back until tomorrow afternoon."

"That's a small amount of time to wait for such good news," said Gwen.

"I think we should pray," said John.

Gwen, Tony, and Rose all turned in unison and looked at John and then looked at one another. They never thought they were ever going to hear John say those words again. John understood their surprise and managed a smile. He closed his eyes, bowed his head, and held out both hands. John, Gwen, Tony, and Rose stood in a small circle and held hands. Thank the Lord, thought Gwen, as tears flowed down her face. John began to pray.

CHAPTER 15

CHAOS

After appearing at the W.O.R.D. event, Simon kept a low profile. Though his exploits had been broadcast all over the world, only a select few, including a few police officers, would remember him. To Lieutenant Perkins only, Simon had become the most wanted person in Louisville, Kentucky. However, because of his exploits, people acted as if it was judgment day. Believers rejoiced, while atheists trembled. Simon watched in obscurity as Jesus Christ was on the lips and minds of everyone in the world. Simon could not help but think of the Scripture that stated that every knee would bow, and every mouth would confess Jesus Christ as Lord. He smiled, thinking that he just might be the tool that Jesus uses to fulfill that passage. He enjoyed watching the world try to explain away the miracles they had just witnessed with the tsunami in Japan.

The media was relentless in covering the miracles. They tried to report from every angle imaginable, and they had been successful in capturing the world's attention. Before it was all said and done, there was at least a thirty-day timeframe in which you could not turn on a television, radio, or cell phone without seeing, hearing, or reading something about the Japan Miracles. Almost every magazine around the world, including sports, agriculture, and fashion, ran an article covering the Japan Miracles.

Every television reporter and radio host who had covered the W.O.R.D broadcast was struggling to explain what they had seen. However, Simon's name was never mentioned, his picture nor his words ever appeared on any broadcast, tape, or film. The reporters were so excited and in awe that they were just babbling during their live broadcast. Reporters started pulling people off the street, or wherever they were, and asking them about their personal text from Jesus. Some shared their message, some didn't, and others didn't want to talk about it at all.

The centuries-old debate about Christianity had been raised to a new level. Was Jesus Christ resurrected from the dead, and was he God in human form when he walked the earth? Whether you believed or not became more important than ever. The Japan Miracles were causing everyone to take a close look at themselves. If Christ is real, am I going to make it to heaven? If He's not, how do you explain the Japan Miracles?

For the next six months, all of Japan was inundated with media personnel. They wanted to get firsthand information directly from those who were caught up in the catastrophe that had transpired on that unforgettable weekend. They talked to people from every walk of life, from the down-and-out homeless person to the penthouse millionaire. They all gave their point of view of what it was like before, during, and after the tsunami. The media was relentless in their coverage and even embellished a few stories, but the public couldn't get enough of it. The Japan Miracles were media gold.

Meanwhile, the religious and scientific communities were extremely busy trying to explain what the world had seen on live television. Almost everything that they believed or had been taught their entire lives was now under a microscope. The leaders of these communities had a lot on the line. Not only were their reputations at stake but so were their livelihoods.

Church offices and synagogues were inundated with phone calls. A lot of people were calling their pastors, priests, and all type of clergy and religious leaders and questioning them about the recent events. Every faith that taught or worshiped anything other than Jesus Christ was being compared to the Japan Miracles. The non-Christian community was asking their god for miracles to be performed before their eyes, like the ones they witnessed in Japan. They wanted proof that their god was just as powerful as Jesus.

This was happening all over the world, and the media was always close by. After a while, the media began lumping all these other worshipers together and calling them non-Christians. The various religious leaders around the world were getting very upset with the media for not identifying them by their beliefs. They were now being identified by what they did not believe as if they were an anomaly. As a result, they were starting to lose their identity and their followers.

The Christian religion started to see a growing increase of members, and they put a huge distance between Christianity and the Nation of Islam. Churches were packed every day their doors were open for any type of service, whether it was a regular church service, a Bible study, or a prayer meeting. As the congregations grew, the churches had to add services. Baptismal pools stayed full as dozens of people joined church every week. People were acting as if the world might end the next day. A lot of ministers capitalized on this fear by preaching sermons from the book of Revelations.

The Christian church experienced a huge growth period for six months after the Japan Miracles, and then things slowly started to return to the way they were. The media hype started to fade, and the fad followers started to separate from the true believers.

The scientific community was working feverishly to discredit the Japan Miracles. They were leaving no stone unturned trying to explain what actually happened that disastrous morning on that Japanese island. The American Association for the Advancement of Science orchestrated the investigation right after it happened. As an international nonprofit organization with thousands of members, they decided to send different teams to look into the alleged miracles on the island of Honshu.

They established a base in Tokyo and tried to determine if the underwater earthquake that caused the tsunami really happened. Scientists and seismologists from all over the world gathered on the island to study the seismology reports and to take a look at the actual site where the quake allegedly happened. They double-checked every seismic machine to make sure it was working properly. They examined the time and dates on the reports to make sure they coincided with the actual date and times recorded by the media. To their dismay, it all checked out. All the machines were working perfectly, and all the reports appeared to be accurate.

The next step was to personally visit the fault line. They brought in professional divers, a sixty-foot boat, a couple of mini-submarines, expensive cameras, amphibious drones, and a lot of other expensive, high-tech equipment. Since the dive was going to be pretty deep, they planned to send down the amphibious drones, which had cameras built into them. They would control the drones from the boat, and anything that showed up on their cameras would be recorded and stored on the equipment in the boat. They would deploy the mini submarines only if the drones couldn't capture the pictures they needed.

The first dive was scheduled at dawn on a Tuesday morning. It was a cold morning, but the temperature was well within the capability of the drones. The scientists gently placed each drone on the surface of the water and started it remotely. The drones jetted effortlessly across the surface of the water for a few yards before they started to dive. Within seconds, they were completely submerged and being tracked by radar.

The scientists estimated that the fault line was a thousand feet deep below them. The drones could function up to fifteen hundred feet, so the depth wasn't a problem. It would take about twenty minutes for the drones to dive a thousand feet. The crew of six drank coffee and made small talk as they waited for the drones to reach the desired depth. Everything was fine as they watched the ocean come alive before their eyes. The cameras on the drones were very clear, although the deeper the drones dived, the darker the picture became. The remote operators turned on the lights on the drones, and that helped tremendously.

The drones soon reached the programmed depth of nine hundred and fifty feet. They leveled off, and their lights pointed downward, looking for the fault. After a few unsuccessful minutes, the monitor started to darken. The lights on the drones soon became useless. All light in the area had been completely engulfed by darkness. The remote operators had to guide the drones by radar. This was extremely difficult, and they debated whether to keep going, bring the drones back, or hold them in one spot and hope that whatever was causing the darkness was temporary.

The remote operators held the drones steady and started maneuvering their cameras. They had no success until the cameras were rotated one hundred and eighty degrees. The cameras picked up a little light and a few fish. The picture was still very fuzzy but better than it had been. The remote operators rotated the cameras back to their previous position and experienced total darkness once again. They rotated the drones from right to left in a full circle hoping to pick up something on the camera. It was so dark that the cameras on the drones did not even pick up each other, and they were only eight feet apart.

The operators slowly moved the drones forward with caution. Again, the operators were driving blind. They lowered the drones another hundred feet in hopes of dropping below whatever was causing the extreme darkness. This didn't help, and the crew was running out of ideas. While they were discussing what to do next, one of the crew glanced at the monitor and witnessed a frightening sight. He called out to the rest of the team and told them to look at the monitor. According to the radar, the two drones were spiraling downward in a clockwise motion. The remote operators tried to regain control of the drones, but they were caught in an underwater whirlpool, known as a maelstrom, and were being pulled down to the bottom of the ocean. They soon disappeared completely from the radar. The crew was speechless. Usually, a maelstrom strong enough to suck those drones under would be visible on the surface of the water, but this one wasn't. None of them had ever encountered anything like this before.

After a couple of days of discussion and planning, the scientists and seismologists decided to try plan B. They would deploy both mini-submarines and enhance their lights by creating a high beam that could pierce the darkness that paralyzed the drones. One sub would stay about fifty feet behind the other, on its port side, for safety reasons.

At dawn on Friday morning, they launched the mini subs, each one carrying four people. They stayed on the surface of the water until they reached the spot in which the drones submerged. The first sub dived, and the second one waited ten seconds before going down. They were cautious not to dive too fast, and they checked and double-checked all their equipment as they descended. Everything was working perfectly.

After only five minutes at their desired depth, the first minisub stopped, and the second one followed suit. The crew of the first minisub radioed the second one and instructed it to come up alongside it. The crews of both were speechless as they looked on in awe. They found the fault line and wondered how they missed it with the drones. Then they realized that the cameras and lights of the drones were pointed down. The fault was so huge that when the drones were directly over it, the cameras were pointed down inside the crevice, which was completely dark.

The reading on their equipment was off the charts. The crevice was so large that the seismologist reports did not accurately measure it. A crevice of this size should have caused total destruction of the entire island, along with a couple of adjoining islands. The mini-sub crews decide to split up and travel along each side of the crevice.

They agreed to make contact with each other every two minutes.

They did not want to travel in the middle of the crevice because of what happened to the drones. If there were maelstroms out there, the minisubs could very easily be in jeopardy. They were not sure how wide or how long the crevice was, but they planned to find out. After an hour underwater, they decide to head back to shore before they ran out of fuel. When they returned to Tokyo, they compared notes and discovered that they had just witnessed a miracle, which was a term scientist never used.

After a few days of going over all the data, the scientists were baffled. They were speechless. They checked, double-checked, and even triple- checked everything, and it still didn't make sense to them. The size of the fault was so large that it looked as if the ocean floor had just opened up. According to their instruments, the crevice was at least five miles wide at its widest point. They weren't sure how long the crevice was because they were running low on fuel before they could measure its entire length. They decided to try to get a full-size submarine to finish their exploration of the crevice.

The size of the crevice indicated that waves at least three times as large as the ones that were recorded could have been created, and they could have pushed at least fifty miles inland into Asia. They didn't understand what was keeping the crevice from turning into a giant vortex and sucking everything within a hundred miles down into it.

While they waited to secure a full-size submarine, another team of scientists was examining the buildings on the island that were supposedly destroyed and rebuilt in a matter of minutes. They examined the entire area looking for evidence that the large waves actually hit the island. They couldn't find any salt-water residue on anything—not on automobiles, buildings, trees, bicycles, not anything. This team was ready to label the tsunami destruction as a hoax until two very significant facts that they could not explain were brought to their attention.

First, all the buildings that were supposedly destroyed and reconstructed were a little different. Their design was not the same as before, both inside and out. It was not really noticeable unless you were familiar with the original structure. For example, each building had an extra floor now, the floor plan was different, and the elevator was on the opposite side of the building. The team of scientists didn't believe this until they were shown blueprints of the buildings. They also examined pictures that had been taken inside and outside the hotels before they were destroyed. The pictures verified how the buildings looked before they were destroyed by the tsunami. Even though they saw the pictures, the scientists still weren't completely convinced because the pictures could be fake.

However, what they saw on the top of a twenty-story hotel shook them to their core. Quite a few of the hotel residents had been complaining of a terrible smell. Hotel management verified that there was a foul odor, but they couldn't isolate its origin. After checking everywhere with no success, the general manager decided to go to the roof. The smell was almost unbearable, and he felt as if he was going to pass out from the stench. Before his eyes lay the carcass of a seventy-five-foot humpback whale, weighing approximately one hundred tons. After the initial shock wore off, the general manager began to panic. He did not know how he could remove this giant carcass or how long it would be before it fell through the roof. He called the fire department and then went to find the scientists.

The scientists were stunned, to say the least. Not even the best magician could have pulled off this stunt without being seen. The animal was too large, and it would have taken large equipment to be able to lift it unless it was lowered to the roof by a helicopter, which was highly unlikely. The general manager had his own theory, which the scientists didn't want to hear.

"God did this on purpose," said the general manager, "because he knew there would be doubters like you. This place has been crawling with media and scientists twenty-four hours a day since the storm ceased. There is no way that whale could have been placed on the roof without using helicopters or setting up massive equipment, which would have taken a few days. Somebody would have seen something."

The scientists were speechless. They had no answers. They took pictures of the carcass and the redesigned buildings. They made copies of the before pictures of the buildings and took their own pictures for comparison purposes. They collected as much evidence as they could before they left Japan. Their final report offered no explanation of the whale on top of the building or the redesign of the reconstructed buildings, at least not one the science community wanted to reveal.

In addition to the religious and science communities, teams of medical specialists were sent to examine the people who were resurrected. They were not sure what they were looking for, but they would know if anything in the victims' bodies were unusual. They would do complete physicals, including drawing blood, taking skin samples, running x-rays and brain scans, checking DNA, and every other test they could think of. They would compare what they found with the previous medical records of the people they examined. This team was twice as large as the others because it included specialists who would only work in their field of expertise when they performed the examinations.

They arrived in Tokyo within twenty-four hours after the W.O.R.D. broadcast ended. A local hospital made arrangements for them to set up their base there and to start examining people as soon as possible. To avoid resistance, they offered free health screenings for anyone who had been resurrected. Most of the volunteers would not have participated if they knew that these specialists were trying to prove that miracles didn't exist.

Things were going as predicted, and nothing unusual was discovered. They thought that there should at least be a few dead blood cells if the body had died, but they did not find one dead blood cell in anyone. Things got interesting when they started doing x-rays. At first, it was just another boring day of testing, and then it happened. The x-ray of a forty-five-year-old man showed that he had no kidneys. The doctor thought that the machine was malfunctioning or that something had blocked that part of the man's body and prevented them from getting a complete picture. The doctor checked the machine, which appeared to be working properly. He took another x-ray and got the same result. He was perplexed, to say the least, so he showed the pictures to his colleagues and swore that the machine was working properly.

All the medical specialists stopped their individual testing and started performing x-rays on as many of the resurrected as they could. They made sure to thoroughly document each person, including contact information, and drew blood samples from each one as well. When they had finished, they had x-rayed 120 people. Forty-seven of the x-rays did not identify a kidney in the person x-rayed. The medical team checked and double-checked everything. They took x-rays of each other just to make sure the machine was functioning properly.

Next, they analyzed the blood samples. They looked at the samples of those who were not showing a kidney. They tested the blood for excessive waste and other particles that the kidneys clean from the blood. They found the blood samples to be perfectly clean as if the kidneys were functioning properly. The team called the forty-seven back a few days later and collected additional blood samples. This time they asked each one if they had ever had problems with their kidneys or had been on dialysis. None of them had ever had kidney problems, and again their blood was perfectly clean.

This was medically impossible. Everything the doctors knew about the human body and the function of the kidney suggested that a person could not live long without their kidneys or dialysis. Yet, these forty-seven people were doing just that. The doctors didn't understand how the blood was being cleaned, and how their body fluids were being balanced, which was also a function of the kidneys.

From that moment on, the medical specialists focused solely on the forty-seven and did not continue testing the others. They determined that the only way to make sure that they didn't have a kidney was to open one of them up. The problem was finding a volunteer who was willing to go under the knife just to satisfy their curiosity. It was more than just curiosity; it was a medical miracle in which they needed first-hand proof. They would film the entire procedure, but no one volunteered. None of the forty-seven believed their kidneys were missing, and even if they were gone, they felt fine.

When the doctors were about ready to give up, a man came forward to volunteer, but he wanted to be paid. He was one of the homeless people and he saw an opportunity to make some money. The doctors were willing to compensate the man, but he was asking for too much. The doctors tried to negotiate a price with the homeless man without him sensing their desperation. They made him one last take-it or leave-offer. Finally, the man relented, and the doctors prepared him immediately for surgery. It took less than an hour for the team to open him up only to discover that the x-ray machine was indeed functioning properly. The man had no kidneys. They filmed the entire surgery and planned to review it more closely later. After they closed him up and the anesthesia had worn off, they told the man that the surgery was a success.

The team of medical specialists went back to the drawing board. They started retesting the forty-seven people. Since they had no kidneys, something else had to be taking over the function of the kidneys. They discussed how they could find out without being extremely invasive. The type of test they wanted to perform was very invasive and included taking biopsies. They needed to come up with a plan. In the meantime, they worked on separating the x-rays of the forty-seven from everyone else. While doing this, one of the specialists came across an x-ray that sent chills through his body. His hands started to shake, and he screamed for his colleagues, who came running. They had been so busy checking the x-rays for kidneys that they failed to examine the entire x-ray. The medical specialists were now looking at an x-ray of a man who had no heart.

CHAPTER 16

CONVERSION

Many stories came out of Japan about the miracles that people were experiencing. The people who shared their stories were diverse. The best stories came from those who had been resurrected and rescued from the rubble. Some of them recalled the moment right up to their death. Some saw their demise coming but couldn't do anything to stop it. Others didn't remember anything but the storm. They had to see it on the news before they realized what had happened. It was like they had gone to sleep and had awakened to what they thought was a dream.

The most compelling story of all came from a Louisville, Kentucky journalist who had been contacted by a local resident about his story. This businessman had purposely scheduled to leave on a business trip to Japan while the W.O.R.D. event was going on. He wanted to get away from the hustle and bustle that he knew would consume Louisville. He was an atheist who was only mildly interested in the event, and he knew that he would be able to watch it on television. He was more interested in ridiculing the religious fanatics than hearing what they had to say.

Darryl Little arrived in Tokyo a few days before the conference began, and he planned to stay a few days after he had completed his business. He wanted to experience the culture before he went back home. Soon after he landed, seismologists started predicting that an earthquake would hit the very island on which he was staying. Later that evening, all radio and television stations were announcing warnings that a minor earthquake would strike Tokyo, where the island of Honshu was located, in a couple of days. They downplayed the warnings as nothing to be overly concerned about. Darryl had been in a similar situation in Los Angeles when the city experienced tremors from a minor quake. The local weathermen there did a great job of providing accurate information to the residents and even made a special effort to reach out to visitors of the city to calm their fears. Darryl figured this would be a similar experience.

Darryl slept well Friday night and did some sightseeing on Saturday. Before he could return to his hotel room for the evening, every local radio and television station was sounding off emergency warnings and informing the island's residents of a major upgrade in the strength and size of the quake. They were also issuing tsunami warnings because the earthquake would be a major one and was advising everyone to take cover. Unfortunately, the warning came too late for the islanders to do anything but hunker down. Panic spread quickly, and even the first responders were not sure how to prepare for the imminent disaster. The island did not have time to successfully execute an exit plan. Authorities had closed the airport to all incoming and outgoing flights. They weren't allowing ships to leave or enter the harbor, and any ships headed toward Japan were rerouted.

When Darryl reached his hotel room, he immediately turned on his television. Every station was covering the terrible situation the island would soon experience, and each station's prediction was more severe than the previous station. His hotel room phone rang, startling him. His wife was calling him to see if he was okay. She had heard about the dire forecast in Tokyo despite all of the W.O.R.D.-related topics that were being broadcast by the news in Louisville. He told her that he was fine for now but that the worse of it was supposed to hit

Sunday morning, which would be Saturday night in Louisville. He did his best to assure her that he would be fine, though he wasn't so sure that he would be. Darryl watched the updates about the earthquake and tsunami until he fell asleep.

The next morning started out calm and serene, but that would soon change. Darryl took a shower, got dressed, and called for room service, but no one in that department answered. He called the front desk, but no one answered there either. A sick feeling came over him as he remembered the disaster warnings and walked toward his hotel room window. He saw that the ocean waters looked rough, really rough. Fifty-foot waves were already crashing onto the empty beach. Darryl's peripheral vision caught something going on below, so he looked straight down from his window. Several people were gathered on the streets, and they seemed to be in distress. He quickly glanced around and soon realized what was going on. Those people were homeless, and no one was allowing them to seek shelter in their building. He could see people pulling on door handles and knocking on doors to no avail.

Darryl was sad, scared, and hungry. He remembered that he had brought some chicken and rice back last night and placed it in the small hotel refrigerator. He pulled it out and heated it in the microwave. That satisfied his hunger for the moment, and he began to wonder about the earthquake warnings. At that moment, he felt the first tremor. He sat on his bed, picked up the remote, and turned on the television. He watched the earthquake and tsunami updates all morning; often distracted by the rattling of the windowpanes and the increasingly more severe tremors.

After a while, there was a break in the news to update everyone on the W.O.R.D. event, which about to start in Louisville, Kentucky. Darryl had forgotten all about it and decided to see if he could find coverage of it on another station since it was being broadcast live all over the world. He thought it would take his mind off of his immediate danger in Honshu. After a few minutes of channel surfing, he was able to find the live broadcast. He was interested to see if the religious world was using the same old arguments to try to convert people to their religion. He couldn't think of a more entertaining way to spend his Sunday morning.

The tremors and the waves were growing significantly worse as he watched the program He ran to his window when he heard a sudden crashing noise outside. To his surprise, giant waves were hitting land and damaging everything in its path. The noise that he had heard was a small building that had just been destroyed by a wave. He noticed that the streets were already flooded and that the homeless people were being swallowed up. Darryl returned to his bed to watch the program, as scared as he had ever been. He was speechless when he saw what was happening in Honshu on the screens in Louisville. Darryl had tuned in to the W.O.R.D event, but the audience at that event was watching the catastrophe in Honshu. He saw the religious representatives on stage looking up at the large screens, but he had no recollection of seeing Simon. He soon realized that he was simultaneously watching his plight on live television as well as out of his hotel room window.

As Darryl Little watched a ten-story building begin to crumble on the television, he heard a thunderous crash. He stood up, looked out the window, and saw the building that he had just seen on television, crumbling before his eyes. A tidal wave had not directly hit that building, so the earthquake must have been responsible for its demise. He saw people being swept away and cars and trucks being tossed around like toys. The tremors became so bad that Darryl could barely stand. He laid across his bed and continued to watch the live broadcast from Louisville. He preferred watching the live broadcast from Louisville instead of the cable channel weather alerts. Watching the live audience react to what he was going through had truly captured his attention.

Then it happened. For the first time since his junior high school years, Darryl entertained the slightest notion that maybe there was a

God. At first, he reasoned that it was fear grabbing a hold of him and telling him that he needed to believe anything to stay alive. He tried to dismiss that idea because he had seen terrible storms before. He just happened to be caught in the middle of this one. But this storm was different, and it wasn't just because he was in the middle of it. He would swear that he felt a distinct power in the middle of this one.

Tears flowed down Darryl's face as he continued to watch the live broadcast. He saw a humongous tidal wave coming straight for his hotel. He quickly turned toward the window and saw the sky darken. His life flashed before his eyes, just as people who have faced near-death experiences have said it would. However, usually, people experienced good memories of family and friends and other good times. However, Darryl's life-flashing moments were different. He thought about all the times he had ridiculed and berated people who believed in God, or Jesus, or the Holy Spirit. He recalled the time that he walked out of church when he was thirteen years old and has never gone back. He remembered the time when, as a college sophomore, he took a New Testament class just to find out what lies and myths they were teaching in an institution of higher learning. Darryl thought about all the times he had denied God. Then, right before the giant tidal wave, coupled with the ferocious tremors, destroyed the hotel in which he was staying, he heard himself mumble two words: "I'm sorry!"

Darryl had become emotional all over again. The reporter offered him a box of tissue and allowed him some time to collect himself before asking him to continue his story. Darryl grabbed a couple of tissues and dabbed at his eyes. After another minute or so, he had regained his composure.

"What happened next?" asked the reporter.

"The next thing I remember is hearing my phone ring."

"The hotel phone?" asked the reporter.

"No," said Darryl, "my cell phone, which was lying on the bed beside me. It was as if I were having a bad dream and my alarm clock was waking me up. But it wasn't an alarm clock. It was the ring tone of my cell phone. I looked over at it and saw that it was exactly 11:25. Then I noticed that I had a text message, and I paused a minute before I read it.

"Why did you pause?" asked the reporter.

"I paused because everything started coming back to me. I remembered seeing the destruction of Honshu, both on the television and out of my hotel room window. I recalled hearing my own voice sounding broken and frightened right before everything came crashing down on top of me. I remembered everything. I opened the text message, thinking it was my wife checking on me to see if I was still alive. To my surprise, it was a message from Jesus. I didn't believe it at first, but I do now."

"What did the text say?"

"It said, "I heard your apology, and you are forgiven." Then it said, "I love you and was signed the Lamb of God."

"Why do you believe that message was sent from Jesus?" asked the reporter.

"Well, first, I was the only one in my room when I died, so no one else could have heard me say that I was sorry. Second, I have watched the replay of the W.O.R.D. event at least a half dozen times and have read many articles about it. I've seen the hotel I was staying in destroyed each time. Then I saw it raised each time. Everyone around the world received a text message from Jesus at exactly the same time. You even said that you received a message, and you can't explain it."

"Yes, I did receive one," said the reporter, "but there has to be a reasonable explanation."

"There is, but a lot of people, including you, don't believe the explanation is reasonable. Many scientists and religious leaders have been trying to say that the Japan Miracles didn't really happen, but there is proof that it did. The media has shown some videos from cameras on the island that should have been impossible to record. The time and date on the video matched exactly with the time and date of the destruction that occurred on the island. That shouldn't have been possible because all power had been knocked out on that part of the island due to the storm. Do you have an answer for these things?"

"No, sir, I don't," said the reporter.

"Well, I do. Jesus is the answer," said Darryl Little.

"What now?" asked the reporter. "Where do you go from here? What do you say to the people who are still not believers?"

"First, I will tell the nonbelievers to open their eyes as I have. Thousands of professionals and so-called experts are trying to explain away the Japan Miracles, but they can't. They say there has to be a reasonable explanation, but they refuse to believe that God is the reason. People are always asking for Old Testament type-miracles, such as the ones that happened in the time of Moses. But when one occurs, people credit it to everything but God. I bet everyone on the island of Honshu believes in God now, even if they didn't believe before. Why do we have to go through a life-or-death experience before we believe?"

"Good question," answered the reporter. "I think it's because a lot of people, such as the science community that you referred to, don't believe in miracles. They need to try to find an explanation for the things they don't understand."

"I believe the Japan Miracles were more than just storm-related miracles," said Darryl. "Just like the birth and the death of Christ. I believe that the Japan Miracles will be a point of reference for every significant piece of Christian history from now on, especially where Japan is concerned. People and the media will point out that this religious event happened two months before the Japan Miracles, or that religious event happened exactly one year after the Japan Miracles."

"That's an interesting concept. I never thought about that."

"The resurrection of the people and the buildings, the pulling back of the giant waves, and the earthquake stopping so the buildings could be resurrected were not the only miracles to come out of Japan during that horrendous tsunami. They are the most obvious miracles, but I think there's a miracle just as big that has been completely overlooked."

"Really, what other miracle have we missed?" asked the reporter.

"Out of all the dozens, maybe hundreds, of story angles that the media has reported, not once have I read or heard a story reporting one of the biggest miracles of all attributed to the Japan Miracles. No one has covered the fact that everyone on the planet is talking about God. Whether they are a believer or a nonbeliever, everyone is contemplating that age-old question of whether or not there is a God. It was all brought about by the international broadcast of the W.O.R.D. event, which was the vehicle used to show the Japan Miracles to the world."

"That's a great point," said the reporter. What a great angle! I should have thought of that." He immediately pulled out his cell phone and made a note to himself to follow up on that angle. "That would be a great story," said the reporter, "so don't mention it to anyone else." Darryl smiled and shook his head.

"As far as where I go from here," Darryl continued, "first, I will devote my life to Christ by attempting to change the mind of nonbelievers. I just have to figure out exactly how I will do that. I know I will start by reading the bible. Then my family and I will find a good Christian church to attend. After that, I am depending on God to lead me."

"That's a remarkable turnaround for a person who ridiculed believers a little more than two weeks ago. What would you like the readers to get from your story?"

"I agree; it is a major change from the person I was two weeks ago. I'm not that person anymore, and I apologize for any harm I have caused to anyone. I pray I did not cause anyone to stumble in their faith."

"It sounds as if you have already been reading the bible," said the reporter.

"I have been. I have spent the majority of my life criticizing believers. But whatever time I have left, I will spend trying to change the minds of the nonbelievers. To answer your question, I would like for whoever reads this article to know that the power and the miracles of Jesus are real."

"That's a powerful statement."

"It's a true statement. The Japan Miracles sent a message and a warning. Jesus has shown us a glimpse of his unequaled power and his ability to conquer death. I am so glad and blessed that I did not die as a nonbeliever. I was given another chance, and I will make the most of it. You may not be as fortunate as I am. I died, was brought back to life, and am now a believer. If you believe in any other explanation for the Japan Miracles other than God, then you are probably lost for all eternity."

"I have heard about all of the miracles that have occurred since the earthquake and tsunami hit Japan," said the reporter, "but what makes you so sure that Jesus was sending the world a message? What is it that has convinced you of this?"

"You have been speaking to a true miracle for the last two hours, without even knowing it. Not only was I resurrected from the dead, but I was resurrected without a heart."

The reporter looked at Darryl as if he had a third eye in the middle of his forehead. Up until that moment, he considered him believable and credible. Now he was thinking that he had wasted two hours talking to someone who was mentally challenged. Trying hard not to sound sarcastic, he continued his questioning.

"Excuse me, will you repeat that?"

"You heard me correctly. I was resurrected from the dead, but I have no heart in my chest. According to doctors, a person cannot live without a heart, unless he or she is hooked up to a machine that duplicates the functions of the heart. I guess you can consider me the walking dead."

"You're serious, aren't you?"

"I am dead serious. No pun intended. You are the first person outside the medical community to hear about this, but I imagine the world will know soon. Teams of scientists came to Japan after Jesus restored the island of Honshu. One of those teams was from the medical community, and they ran tests on just about everyone who had been resurrected."

"Are you saying that those doctors told you that you have no heart, and you believe them?"

"Yes, I believe them because they showed me the x-rays of my chest. They even went a step further and allowed me to watch them take x-rays of each other to prove that the machine was working properly. After they had taken x-rays of each other, they then took another x-ray of my chest. Nobody reprogrammed the machine or made any adjustments to the equipment. Their x-rays showed a heart in their chest, but mine showed an empty cavity where my heart should have been."

"I think they were pulling your leg in some way," said the reporter.

"You have to take into consideration the purpose of their mission," said Darryl. "They were from the American Association for the Advancement of Science, and they don't believe in God. Their mission was to disprove the idea of miracles by giving a scientific explanation for the things that most people can't explain. A man walking around without a heart has to be considered a miracle, which can only be attributed to God. A group of specialists, top in their fields, telling the world that I am a walking miracle is against everything they believe and contradicts their life's work. That would be the last thing they would do unless they were absolutely sure it was true."

"That part sounds believable," said the reporter. "However, I must take the side of the science community on this one. A person cannot live independently without a heart. The only way to be 100 percent sure is to open you up and take a look."

"They did that too," said Darryl, as he opened his shirt and showed the reporter his scar. "Like you, they wanted proof and so did

I, so I allowed them to open me up and take a look."

"This is crazy! This can't be true!

"The doctors will announce it to the world soon enough, with video to verify it. I am one of many miracle survivors. There are forty-seven people who were resurrected without kidneys, and they are all doing just fine. However, I am the only resurrected survivor who doesn't have a heart."

"This is getting a little weird," said the reporter. "This sounds like something out of a sci-fi movie."

"I guarantee you that everything I have told you is absolutely true. It was hard for me to believe also, even after the doctors opened me up. However, my confirmation came straight from God."

"Are you going to tell me you had an Old Testament type of vision?"

"Something like that," said Darryl. For the first time in my adult life, I have to admit to myself that there is a higher power out there somewhere. A person just can't walk around under their own power without a heart or kidney. To me, it is beyond the scope of possibility of being a coincidence. Also, for the first time in many years, I want to talk to God. I have questions that need to be answered."

"I assume this is the part where you tell me that God spoke to you?"

"Yes, it is, but why do you say that so sarcastically? Are you a nonbeliever?"

"I believe in God, but some of the things you have told me are hard to swallow."

"I understand that you are like most people. You believe what you want to believe."

"There may be some truth to that," said the reporter, "but you have to know how insane some of this sounds. Talking freely about walking around under your own power and without physically having a heart in your body will get you a one-way ticket to a mental health facility."

"I admit that my story is hard to believe, but it's all true. Anyway, getting back to my confirmation, God did speak to me. He knew my thoughts, and He told me why He took my heart. To make a long story short, God told me that I wasn't using my heart, so I might as well not have one."

"Wow, that's pretty rough," said the reporter.

"Yes, it is, and you can imagine how I felt. I had denied God my entire life and ridiculed believers at every opportunity. God told me that He is love, and if I didn't believe in love, then I shouldn't have a heart. God also told me there was another reason for taking my heart and for taking the kidneys of those forty-seven people."

"What is the other reason?"

"God knew that there would always be nonbelievers, but God has a way of bringing them around, at least some of them, and that is through miracles. You see the smarter humans get and the more they accomplish, the less they think they need God."

"I think I understand what you're saying," said the reporter. "God has changed the rules of science as far as the human body is concerned. God is using you and those people without kidneys as examples of what's possible with God."

"That's correct, but God has also given us another reason to believe. That's not the end of the story."

"I'm dying to hear the rest."

"God told me that I can earn my heart back."

"Is God asking you to be a pastor?"

"I don't think so. I think God is just asking me to believe in Christianity, to persuade others to do the same and to live as the Bible instructs us. I think when I have accomplished these things, God will give me my heart back. I also think that will take a while."

"It sounds as if you have made up your mind to follow God," said the reporter.

"Yes, I have. Now my mission is to convince others to do the same."

CHAPTER 17

FAITH REWARDED

John and Gwen arrived at the hospital at about noon on Monday. Rose and Tony had spent the night as usual. Trey was happy that he would be going home. All day Sunday he went from one test to the next. His team of doctors was bewildered by his recovery. They could come to only one conclusion: It appeared that the procedure was working. After thorough testing, Trey still showed traces of the disease, but his organs and blood were showing a significant reduction of the abnormal protein. The doctors scheduled Trey for follow-up treatments, but they remained highly optimistic about his future.

Though he had been at the hospital for only a few days, Trey was treated like royalty when he was released. Doctors, nurses, administrative personnel, and even a few housekeeping and maintenance workers stopped by Trey's room to say goodbye and to wish him well. He received cards, balloons, stuffed animals, and plenty of candy during his hospital stay. Trey had an entourage following him as he was wheeled through the hallways, down the elevator, and out to the main exit. Everyone hugged and kissed him before he left, and he was enjoying every minute of it.

Rose fastened Trey into his car seat, while Tony loaded all his gifts into the trunk of their car. John and Gwen thanked the hospital personnel and then got into their car and prepared to follow Tony and

Rose home. Trey smiled as he waved goodbye to all of the hospital well-wishers. He was full of energy and talked and asked questions about everything he saw on the way home. Tony and Rose could tell that he was feeling better. Both of them, along with John and Gwen, had taken off work the entire week to spend time with Trey. He would get as much attention as he could handle this week.

The next few months flew by for the Crenshaw family. Trey was receiving bi-monthly checkups as a routine precaution. He received a few more treatments and was getting stronger and more active by the day. Trey was doing very well, but John caught himself falling back into his old habits.

When he caught himself being negative, he thought about what Simon had told him. He alone could choose to be happy or not. John also remembered the promise that he made to himself: no matter what the future held; he would cherish the moment. This helped to bring him out of his funk. He would force himself to smile, and then he would go play with Trey.

On Wednesday morning, Trey was due for his last scheduled treatment. Tony, Rose, John, and Gwen had gone to every treatment. On this particular day, John got to meet Dr. Richards. As they were waiting for Trey to complete his treatment, Gwen happened to see Dr. Richards pass by the waiting room door. She jumped up and went after him. A few minutes later she came back with Dr. Richards. Gwen was smiling from ear to ear as she introduced him to her family. Gwen was ecstatic because Dr. Richards was wearing the necklace that John had received from his grandmother; the necklace he had given to a small, frightened child over twenty years ago. Gwen had never noticed him wearing it, but she recognized it immediately and knew John would as well. As John and Dr. Richards shook hands Gwen could tell that her husband was struggling with his emotions. John shook hands longer than usual as he stared at the cross around the doctor's neck.

"Let's go check on, Trey," said Gwen. "I think that John and the doctor have a lot to talk about." Tony and Rose got up and followed

Gwen out of the waiting area.

Dr. Richards was not sure what was going on. He had no idea who John was, other than Gwen's husband and Trey's grandfather, and he wasn't sure why the others had left. Dr. Richards assumed that the conversation had something to do with Trey and his treatment.

"That's a very nice cross you're wearing," said John. "Where did you get it?"

"An angel gave it to me when I was a child," replied Dr. Richards.

John was not expecting that answer and had to pause a minute before he could speak again.

"Are you okay?" asked Dr. Richards.

"I am excellent," said John. "I couldn't be better. I was just surprised by that angel comment you just made. It sounds as if there is a story behind the cross."

"Actually, there is," said the doctor, "but it's personal, and it chokes me up sometimes. I'm sure it would only bore you. I thought you wanted to talk to me about Trey. I'm sure that your family didn't leave the room so that we could talk about my necklace."

"Believe it or not, that's exactly why they left the room."

"I don't understand," said Dr. Richards.

"You said that an angel gave you that cross when you were a child. Did it happen to be when you and your father were in a car accident?"

"How did you know about that? I know that my story has been in the local papers, but to my recollection, nothing about this cross was in the article."

"Well," said John, "I was the first one on the scene after you and your father were in that accident. I was the man who tried to calm you down when you were in the backseat crying. I gave you one of my monogrammed handkerchiefs and pressed it against the small cut on your forehead. I let you keep that also. I see that the cut left a small scar."

"That was you?" asked Dr. Richards with excitement. "I don't believe it. I didn't think I would ever meet the person who helped me.

Why didn't you come back so my mom and I could thank you? We were told that someone called the hospital and reported the accident, but no one knew who it was."

"I was ashamed and hurting back then. My son had just died, and I had decided to walk home and deal with my pain the only way I knew how. Your car passed right by me and almost hit me. I was so preoccupied and hurting from my son's death that I never saw it coming."

"I understand," said Dr. Richards, "but what was there to be ashamed of? I heard about your son's death, and I gave blood to help find a cure. Your son's death was not your fault, so why did you feel ashamed?"

"I was ashamed because I was hurting so bad that I walked past you and your father. I was in so much pain that I wanted someone else to hurt like I was hurting. But something deep down inside of me wouldn't let me do it. I turned around and went back to check on you."

"I remember that person as being kind, soft-spoken, and calming. I couldn't make out your face through my tears, but I remember that the person was tall, because he bent down to talk to me. As a matter of fact, I equated that person to Jesus Christ."

"You're pulling my leg, right?" asked John.

At that moment Dr. Richards pulled a handkerchief from his hip pocket. It was the same one that John had left with him so many years ago. Dr. Richards opened the handkerchief up to show the initials. All that could be seen was the letters J and C. John's middle initial had been blotted out by the blood from the cut that Dr. Richards received from the accident.

"You see," began Dr. Richards, "the only initials I saw were J and C, as in Jesus Christ. For the longest time, I held on to this handkerchief and wouldn't let anyone take it from me. I didn't even wash it for at least a year, and that's not an exaggeration. My mother allowed me to hang on to it as sort of a security blanket. She said that it helped with my healing after my father died. I was careful not to get it dirty, but when my mom finally washed it, that bloodstain had set in and wouldn't come out. My mother and I didn't want the stain to come out. She always hand washed it, being careful not to rub out that bloodstain."

"I don't know what to say," said John. "I am sorry that you lost your father. I didn't know that the cross and the handkerchief meant that much to you, but I am glad they were a comfort to you. They meant a lot to me also, but I want you to keep them. My grandmother told me that the day would come when my faith would not be dependent on that cross. Now, I know what she meant."

"Thank you, John. I am sorry for the loss of your son, but I hear the treatment your grandson has been receiving has been very successful. You know that he has been getting partial blood transfusions created from what we learned from your son's blood mixed with mine."

"Yes, I just found that out recently, and I thank you for everything. I hope we can stay in touch beyond hospital visits. If you like high school basketball, I know a coach who would love to get you tickets, if you're interested."

"I would like that," said Dr. Richards.

At that time, Gwen, Rose, and Tony returned to the room. They had good news that they wanted to share with John, and they could hardly wait to do so.

"It looks as if you two had a nice talk," said Gwen. "You two are just chatting away like old buddies."

"We are old buddies," said John. "We haven't seen each other in a long time, and we're catching up on old times."

"That's good to hear," said Gwen. "I have some great news for you, honey."

"If I get any more good news, I will pop from happiness," said John.

"That's exactly how I feel," said Gwen. 'This is so unbelievable that I think I am dreaming. God is so good! I never would have thought in a million years…"

"Go ahead and tell him, Mom," said Rose as she interrupted her mother. "We're growing older by the minute."

"I'm so sorry," said Gwen, "I'm just so excited. First of all, Trey will be here in a minute, and he is doing great. The doctors said that his blood and organs look great and that this will indeed be his last treatment. They still want to see him once a month for the next year to make sure there is no relapse."

"That is great news," said John! "It sounds to me like they are telling us that Trey has been healed. God is good!"

"Not exactly," said Gwen, "but that is what the next year of checkups will determine."

"Tell him the other news," demanded Rose.

"John, the doctors feel so positive about how Trey reacted to the treatment that they think it will lead to a cure. Do you know what this means? Junior's blood was used along with Dr. Richards's to try to find a cure, and now they think they have found it. John, they want to name the new research center that is being built next door after Junior."

John stared at his wife as if he didn't understand what she had said. He didn't know what to say. He knew there was nothing wrong with his hearing, but he never dreamed in a million years that something like this would happen. He just stared at Gwen as tears began to roll down his cheeks.

"The medical building that is being built next door will have Junior's name on it. The hospital administrators want to name it the John Samuel Crenshaw Jr. Research Center. They asked if that was okay, and I told them yes because I knew you would love to have it named after Junior."

Tears started to flow down John's cheeks now. He covered his face with his hands. Gwen didn't expect him to get so emotional. Dr. Richards pulled out his handkerchief and handed it to John. He accepted it and smiled when he saw that it was the one that used to belong to him. John wiped his eyes and tried to regain his composure.

"Are you okay, Dad," asked Rose.

"Yes, baby girl, I'm fine. I was just smacked in the face by my own words but in a very loving and supportive way."

"What are you talking about?" asked Gwen.

"Baby, do you remember me telling you about when I met Simon, you know the guy who appeared at the W.O.R.D. event?"

"Yes, I remember," said Gwen.

"I don't think I told you the last thing I said to him. You see Simon was telling me some things from my past that I had forgotten and didn't want to hear. He was proving that he was who he said he was by telling me things that I had not told anyone else. I knew deep down that this guy was different, but I was so mad that I wasn't hearing him. Simon was telling me that Jesus had been with me throughout my entire life and was trying to convince me not to give up on him."

Dr. Richards had no idea who John and Gwen were talking about. He thought they were referring to a friend of the family and he just listened.

"John, everybody knows how hurt you were. I'm sure he didn't hold whatever you said against you."

"No, I don't think he held it against me, but the news you just told us verifies everything he told me that night. Jesus has been with me all my life. You see the last thing I blurted out to Simon, in anger, was that if Jesus was real, he would heal Trey and he would prove that Junior's death was necessary to make the world a better place."

"Wow!" exclaimed Gwen. "That's pretty powerful."

"It's beyond powerful. There are no words to describe the revelation that just took place and how I feel. I'm just so undeserving," said John

"None of us deserve God's goodness or mercy," said Gwen. "Don't beat yourself up. You were in a bad place, and I am sure that God knew how hurt you were."

"I am good," said John. "I just feel as if I have a lot of catching up to do and a lot of apologies to make."

"Paw-paw, paw-paw!" screamed Trey as he came running up the hall, followed by a couple of nurses.

"Hey, Trey, what took you so long?" asked John as he bent down and picked him up.

"Candy, paw-paw," said Trey.

"That's why he's always running to you," said Gwen. "You have the boy hooked on candy bars."

"Your jealousy is showing," teased John. "I don't have any candy on me, but we'll stop on the way home and get you one. Would that be alright?"

"Okay," said Trey as he grabbed John's hand. "Let's go."

They all laughed and prepared to leave the hospital. John returned the handkerchief to Dr. Richards and promised to stay in touch. They shook hands as Gwen, Tony, and Rose said goodbye to everyone at the nurse's station. Tony moved the car seat from his car to John's since John promised to stop and get Trey candy. Tony and Rose drove off. They would meet John, Gwen, and Trey at home. Trey reminded his grandparents all the way to the store that they promised to stop and get him a candy bar.

Life seemed to be much easier now for everyone. Tony and Rose stayed with John and Gwen for another year until they were able to move into their own house. They were doing well, and their support system was unbelievable. They had met so many people and made so many friends during their visits to the children's hospital.

John and Gwen woke up every morning pinching themselves. After all, they had been through, they often thought they would never lead a normal life again. Life was better than normal. They were thriving, and they were happy. They visited the construction site of the research center at least once a week. After about eight months of construction, they were surprised one day when they visited the construction site and saw that Junior's name had been placed on the building. They got choked up when they tried to read it aloud. The John Samuel Crenshaw Jr. Research Center became a mouth full for them. They hugged each other and stared at the name on the building for twenty minutes, as they talked about how far they had come and how well Trey was doing.

Gwen called Tony and Rose to tell them about the sign, and they were able to visit the site later that same day. They marveled at the name on the building. Rose teared up as she read her brother's name out loud. She became overwhelmed when she tried to talk about the night her brother passed away. Tony held her and told her that everything was okay. He reminded her that Junior would never suffer again and that he was sure that he was smiling down on them. This seemed to calm her as they walked to their car.

Six months later the research center held a ribbon-cutting, grand opening ceremony. The local media covered the event, and there was a huge crowd present. John was already a local celebrity with all of the success he had had with his basketball team. His entire family attended the grand opening along with his team, his friends, almost the entire school, and the surrounding community. It was a great moment for the family, and they were all visibly emotional. After the ribbon-cutting ceremony, the family took a tour of the building and was treated to a nice brunch in the cafeteria. That perfect day was capped off with each family member watching the recap of the ceremony from their home on the six o'clock evening news.

John and Gwen couldn't think of when life had been better. Gwen was so grateful that her husband had once again become the man she had married. She thanked the Lord two or three times a day, every day, for her family. John's change was very visible to everyone who knew him. He had a more positive attitude and appeared more grateful and appreciative for the little things in life. He started attending church again regularly, and he even started teaching a Sunday school class. He led the prayer most of the time for his basketball team before and after each game. John allowed Jesus to lead him in every aspect of his life, and he rarely had a bad day. He had plenty of days that most of us would prefer not to have, but he had trained himself to never spend more than a couple of hours worrying about anything. After he let off a little steam, John turned the situation over to Jesus and asked him for direction. That worked for him, and he loved leaving the tough situations in the hands of Jesus.

CHAPTER 18

UNFINISHED BUSINESS

Simon enjoyed watching the world react to the Japan Miracles. He took delight in seeing the believers recommit themselves to Christ. He enjoyed watching nonbelievers convert and become believers. He took great pleasure in watching the nonbelievers try to scientifically explain the miracles. He chuckled when the general manager found the large whale on the roof of the hotel. It was at that moment that he discovered that Jesus had a sense of humor. However, Simon thought that resurrecting some of the victims without certain organs was genius. The man who didn't have a heart was mind-blowing to everyone, including Simon. Jesus had not told him that some of the resurrected people would be missing vital organs, but he understood the reasoning behind it. God created the human body, and God could redesign it at any time. Humans, with their arrogance and self-proclaimed intelligence, credit their existence to luck and evolution. How will they explain someone walking around without a heart and not give God the credit?

As gratifying as the Japan Miracles were for Simon, they were a huge boost for Christianity. People all over the world were discussing the Father, Son, and Holy Spirit. Simon felt very gratified and very humble that he had been allowed to be a part of this rediscovery.

However, he knew he had more work to do and he focused on the things that Jesus wanted him to accomplish. He was pleased with the things he had already done, and he was most proud of the spiritual growth of John Crenshaw and the rest of his family. It was situations like this that made him very grateful to be a servant of Jesus. He was starting to see the fruits of his labor.

Simon would start by paying a visit to Rodney Peterson. Rodney was the first person in Louisville who made eye contact with him. At the time, he was much more curious about Simon's red hands than he was with his eyes. When Rodney first noticed Simon, he was preoccupied with the Louisville Police Department. Simon drew the interest of the police away from him when he appeared on the scene, and Rodney was able to slip away unnoticed.

Rodney was a handyman and a bit of a jack-of-all-trades. He had converted his garage into his workshop, and his small business had done well up until fifteen months ago. Business had slowed down considerably, and his family was barely getting by. The small jobs had started to dry up, and the large jobs were hard to get. The big companies wanted him to supply proof of his certification or license, but he didn't have those. He didn't mind studying so that he could obtain the certifications or licenses he needed, but as a one-man operation, he didn't have the time. His wife helped him with the business when she could, but she was looking for steady work. She was currently working for a temp agency until she could secure a permanent job. If he went back to school, he would have to turn down work, and things were too tight right now to do that.

Finding work was not Rodney's main concern at the moment. His main goal was staying out of jail. After his run-in with the police, Rodney stayed close to home, but he would sometimes go to a local sports bar at night, just to keep from going stir crazy. He spent most of his time in his workshop. Though he escaped the police before he was identified, he wondered if there were cameras in the area that captured the whole incident. He kept expecting the police to knock on his door at any time, and he was a nervous wreck. He was not sure what he should do. He had never been in trouble with the law before, and he kept watching the local news to see if he was on it.

A couple of days after the W.O.R.D. broadcast, Rodney was having a beer at the local sports bar. However, sports programs were not being broadcast. The world was still obsessed with the Japan Miracles. As Rodney was drinking his beer, the story of Simon's first run-in with the police was rebroadcast. He watched it intensely. He remembered every bit of it as if it had just happened. He was appreciative of the blackout because that's when he escaped. However, one thing was noticeably missing from the broadcast. Rodney was not shown in the story at all. He knew that he had been there, and he witnessed everything that happened. Whoever had filmed that scene should have captured his presence.

"I guarantee you that you not being part of that televised story is not luck," said Simon. "In fact, there is no such thing as luck."

With his beer still in his hand, Rodney quickly spun around to see Simon standing behind him with his hands in his pockets. He became paralyzed with fear. His first thought was to run, but he couldn't run because he was too scared. He took a swig of his beer, and his hand visibly shook as he lifted the bottle to his mouth.

"Do not be afraid," said Simon. "I am not here to hurt you. I see that you recognize me."

"Your picture is being shown all over the world," said Rodney. "Everyone on the planet probably recognizes you."

"If that was true, then everybody in this establishment would be acting similarly to the way you are," said Simon. People remember the deeds that were done, but they will not remember me. Just like your image was not shown when you had an encounter with law enforcement, mine was only seen by a few people when the Japan Miracles were shown. However, my hands are still red and I imagine there would be quite a bit of excitement if I removed my hands from my pockets."

"Oh, you remember my encounter with the police," said Rodney. "I can explain."

"I don't want an explanation," said Simon. "I would like to know how you plan to live your life from this moment forward since you have been given another chance."

"What do you mean another chance?"

"As I said before, your image not appearing in the scene where I was confronted by law enforcement was by design. You do not have to worry about being pursued by the law. You are not in trouble with the law. They are not looking for you. There is no evidence of your crime."

"The police are not looking for me?" asked Rodney. "Are you serious? How can you possibly know that? Never mind," said Rodney after he thought about it. "Why me, why are you helping me?"

"That is my question to you. Have I wasted my time and effort on you?"

"No sir, you haven't. I have never been in trouble with the law before, and it will never happen again. I have learned my lesson. Thank you for your help."

"Jesus is the person you should be thanking. I hope you have learned from that experience. You have a lot of skill and intelligence. Your family needs you. Don't waste your God-given talents."

"You can count on it," promised Rodney, as he placed his beer on the bar. I am going to make time to go back to school. I like technology. I think I will study programming."

"Technology is a good choice, but don't forget to keep Jesus in your life. I will be checking on you, Rodney Peterson. Now I need to go and speak with that officer that you had the encounter with."

Simon turned and walked away. Rodney just stared at him as he walked out into the night. He began to get nervous as he thought over the things Simon had just said. He didn't know what Simon meant when he said that he would be checking on him. He wondered why Simon wanted to talk to the police officer. He was hoping he hadn't changed his mind about giving him another chance. He caught himself starting to stress again, so he took a deep breath. He remembered the promise he had just made moments ago about changing his life. Rodney asked the Lord for strength, courage, and direction and left the bar.

Simon wanted to speak with Lieutenant Perkins, and he knew exactly where he could find him. He would be in his cruiser patrolling the downtown area, not far from where they first met. Simon headed in that direction. This time he wanted to talk to Lieutenant Perkins alone.

On this particular night, there was a concert at the Convention Center. Simon knew that Lieutenant Perkins would stay within a mile radius of that area until the concert was over, just in case a disturbance broke out. Simon was walking down the street when he saw a police cruiser coming his way. He knew it was Lieutenant Perkins. Simon pulled his red hands out of his pockets so that they would be clearly visible. He waited until he knew the Lieutenant had recognized him, and then he ducked into a nearby parking garage. Simon commanded the Lieutenant's communication system not to work so that he couldn't call for backup. He knew the Lieutenant would follow him into the parking garage anyway.

Lieutenant Perkins pulled his car into the entrance of the garage and parked it. He tried to call for backup one more time, but his car radio was not working. He got out of his car and walked outside the garage to see if he could get a signal on the radio connected to his uniform. Again, he was unsuccessful. Lieutenant Perkins removed his pistol from its holster and went back into the garage. He walked slowly and cautiously. He saw a red glare coming from the second level. The garage lights were white, so they could not be the source of the red glare. Simon's red hands were the first thing that came to his mind. He remembered what happened with Simon at the W.O.R.D. event and he was nervous.

As he climbed the steps to the second level, the Lieutenant kept his pistol pointed up toward the top of the steps. He was facing the elevator when he reached the second level. He quickly walked over to it, placing his back against the wall. The Lieutenant slowly peeked around the corner and saw that the red glare was coming from the far end of the garage. He took a longer look and saw Simon standing there as if to be waiting for him. His hands were glowing at his side. The Lieutenant tried to call for backup once more but to no avail. He started to sweat as he pondered whether he should face Simon alone or wait for help. If he went for help, he knew that Simon would be gone before he returned.

"I am waiting on you, Lieutenant," said Simon. "There is no need to be afraid."

"I'm not afraid of you," replied Lieutenant Perkins. "I just want to make sure that my blood does not wind up on your hands."

"I know, that is exactly why you are afraid," said Simon. "Don't worry. I will not harm you. I want to help you."

"What are you talking about? I don't need help with anything. You are a wanted man, and I intend to bring you in one way or the other."

"I am only wanted by you. I am right here. Come and get me."

The Lieutenant slowly walked out to the middle of the floor, pointing his pistol at Simon the entire time. He took a few steps toward Simon and stopped. Simon was still a good eighty feet from him. Simon took a couple of steps forward until he stood directly under a ceiling light. The Lieutenant could now see him clearly.

"We can do this the easy way or the hard way," said the Lieutenant. "You can walk out of here or be carried out in a body bag. It's your choice."

"You are willing to use your weapon on me when I just told you that I am not here to harm you?"

"That's probably the same thing you said to whoever's blood is on your hands."

"I just want to talk to you for a few minutes," said Simon as he walked forward.

"That's far enough," shouted the Lieutenant. "I would hate to shoot you, but I will. You're wanted all over the world. I can drop you right now, and no one will question it. Who are you?"

"The world is not interested in me. Your weapon is of no concern to me. I told you who I am the last time we met when you put your shackles on me. You just don't believe it." Simon continued to walk toward the Lieutenant.

"I'm warning you," said the Lieutenant.

Simon kept coming. The Lieutenant fired twice. Both bullets fell to the concrete floor right in front of Simon, who continued to walk slowly toward the Lieutenant. The Lieutenant fired three more shots. The bullets fell to the floor in front of Simon just as the others had. The Lieutenant was scared. He was visibly shaking. Simon kept coming, and the Lieutenant kept shooting until his pistol was empty. Each bullet followed the previous one to the floor. Simon now stood six feet from the Lieutenant. The Lieutenant held the smoking gun, frozen in fear.

All of the blood left Lieutenant Perkins' face, and his face turned so pale that he looked lifeless. His breathing became shallow, and his heart was racing. The left side of his face began to sag and contort as if he was in pain. Lieutenant Perkins was having a stroke. As he began to slump to the floor, Simon intervened. He ordered the Lieutenant to stand up straight and holster his weapon. The Lieutenant obeyed him. They stood face-to-face, and the Lieutenant was about to pass out.

"Open your eyes!" commanded Simon.

The Lieutenant had no choice but to obey. He didn't know how Simon had taken control of him. He just wished Simon would let him die.

"You will not die here," said Simon. "Breathe!" commanded Simon, and the Lieutenant's body obeyed. Simon ordered the Lieutenant's body into perfect health. He ordered his brain to heal and repair the damage caused by the stroke. He ordered his heart and every organ to work as it should. He ordered all his veins and arteries to have clear pathways, and he ordered all foreign bodies and diseases to leave his body. He ordered the Lieutenant's muscles to be strengthened, and all his faculties and senses to be in perfect working order. Lieutenant Perkins heard everything that Simon said, and he became more alert. He felt his body grow stronger, but he did not yet have control of it. Simon still controlled his body.

"I will release you in a minute," said Simon, "but first you need to listen to me. As I said before, I am not here to harm you. I am here to help you, whether you believe it or not. Your health has been restored not by me but by the mercy and the power of Jesus. You should realize that if I wanted to harm you, nothing is preventing me from doing so right now.

I will say once more that the blood on my hands is not from a crime. It is the life-giving blood of Jesus. You witnessed the Japan Miracles, and you are helpless before me now. You just tried to kill me, and according to the law, I have every right to defend myself, even if it means taking your life. That's not the law I live by anymore, and I haven't for a long time."

Simon released the hold he had on the Lieutenant, who caught himself as his body relaxed. His first reaction was to draw his weapon, but he fought the urge to do so. It would do him no good because the clip was empty. He was sure that Simon would not allow him to reload. The Lieutenant thought about what Simon has just told him as he examined his body. Even some of his minor aches and pains, and scars were gone. The Lieutenant wasn't sure if he believed everything that Simon had told him, but he did believe one thing: Simon could have harmed him if that was his desire. The Lieutenant relaxed a little and decided to hear Simon out.

"Why didn't you let me die?" asked Lieutenant Perkins.

"What would that have accomplished? Besides, I do not have the power over life and death," said Simon. "Only Jesus has that power, and he is not finished with you."

"You're pulling my leg, right? Are you from this world? No one on this planet has the kind of power you have."

"I told you who I am. I have no power at all. I am but a tool in the hand of my master. You have a difficult time believing in Jesus. There was a time, though, when you were a believer."

"You don't know anything about me. If Jesus is real, why didn't he let me die? What did you mean that he is not finished with me?"

"I know everything about you. However, Jesus has not yet revealed to me the plans he has for you."

"What could you possibly know about me?" asked the Lieutenant. "Why did you come looking for me? I don't think that it was luck that I saw you walking down the street right in front of me. What do you want with me?"

"There is no such thing as luck," said Simon. "Jesus wants to restore your faith in Him. You believed in Him when you were young, until your grandfather and your father died. That's when your faith took a blow, and you have still not recovered from it."

Lieutenant Perkins recalled his grandfather and father's deaths. He began to feel the hurt and the pain that he felt when they died. Though they passed away at different times, they both died in the line of duty in a similar fashion. Maybe the Perkins family really does have a curse on them.

"Your family is not cursed," continued Simon.

"You read minds too?" asked the Lieutenant. "Is there anything you can't do? How do you know about my father and grandfather?"

"I can do all things through Jesus," replied Simon. "I told you that I know all about you. I know about your family and what you consider a curse. I know why you have not married and started your own family. It's all because of what you call the Perkins family curse."

"What do you want with me?" asked the Lieutenant through a broken voice.

"You come from a family of law enforcement that goes back for eight generations. I know that none of your relatives retired from law enforcement. They all died in the line of duty, except your sister, and she quit after she was severely wounded. You, Lieutenant Perkins, are waiting for death because you believe in the Perkins family curse. You believe that you, too, will die in the line of duty. That is why you have never married and had kids. You do not want to pass the curse to your offspring."

Lieutenant Perkins hung his head. He could not look Simon in the eyes. Simon was correct. He tried not to think about it so that it wouldn't affect his work, but he always recalled the family curse whenever he was in a tight situation. He always requested backup, even when he was pulling over speeders. He had a very bad feeling when he could not call for backup earlier. The Lieutenant thought that he would fall victim to the Perkins family curse tonight.

"I don't know what to say," said the Lieutenant. "I don't know how you know all of that about me and my family. I think that there was a time when I was a believer, but it's been so long ago I am not really sure. I don't deny Christ. I just don't follow him."

"That is what I want to change," said Simon.

"It's hard for me to follow Christ because I have a hard time believing in Him," said the Lieutenant as he raised his head. "I find it difficult to believe in Him because my family has suffered for generations. I felt obligated to get into a career field that I knew would kill me. I am honored to follow the family tradition, and I like being a police officer, but I am always wondering which bad guy will be the one to take me out and continue the curse. I had a very strong feeling that it was going to be you this evening."

"You can be the one to break the family curse," said Simon, "because it's not real."

"I wish I could believe that."

"Do you know that, except for your sister, the law enforcement members of your family did not believe in Jesus?"

"I knew that my father wasn't a believer."

"It started eight generations ago when the first Perkins died in the line of duty. His son took it hard and cursed God. He lost his faith and taught his children not to believe. This went on from generation to generation. The ironic part is that each female member of the family, wives, and sisters, were believers. There was an internal holy war in the Perkins household. The men denied God, while the women believed and tried to teach about God. Even though the men in your family ended up denying God, they were always introduced to the gospel, so they did have a foundation in Jesus."

"I think I understand what you are telling me.

"Yes, you do. Being in law enforcement is a dangerous job, and an officer needs all the protection he or she can get. Your relatives tried to do it on their own, without Jesus, and so do you. It can't be done."

"You're telling me that the length of my law enforcement career depends directly on my faith in God?"

"I am telling you that man has been given free will, and that our choices can lead to life or death. It is impossible to act counter to what you truly believe. If you believe you will die on the job, that's how you will act. You said yourself that you thought the Perkins curse would be fulfilled tonight by me taking your life. That's how you acted when you came after me with no backup, knowing the things you have seen me do."

"What about my sister? She is a believer like you said, yet she was almost mortally wounded in the line of duty."

"Actually, your sister is very happy and is leading a carefree life. Her decision to leave law enforcement released her from the so-called family curse. If she is not in law enforcement, she doesn't have to worry about dying in the line of duty. Like you, she became an officer out of obligation. It is not what she wanted to do. Because of her faith she prayed and was instructed to use her God-given talents elsewhere. That is why she got out of law enforcement."

"I know what you are asking, and I will give it some thought. It will be hard not to think about it after tonight. I just don't know where to start."

"The beginning is always a good place to start. Talk to Jesus. He will be glad to hear from you."

"That must be what he was telling me on my phone," said the Lieutenant. "I read the message quickly and then forgot about it. I thought it was some type of trick. My text message said that he would love to talk to me about what has been bothering me. He ended it by saying I love you and signed it the Lamb of God."

"You have a personal invitation from Jesus. I think that you should accept it. Remember, Jesus, is not finished with you yet."

Lieutenant Perkins watched Simon as he walked past him, went down the stairs, and stepped out into the night.

CHAPTER 19

BORN AGAIN

As Simon exited the parking garage, he knew where he needed to go next. In fact, he had two more stops to make before the night was over. His first stop would be at a nearby church. He wanted to visit a certain associate pastor there. The church was having a mid-week service, and this associate pastor was the guest speaker. He would be very surprised to see Simon, to say the least. They had met once before, but this time it would be on his terms.

Simon stood in the back of the church because the service was well underway. The choir was singing "Love Lifted Me," and the congregation was singing along and clapping their hands. Pastor Gerald Vincent was sitting in a large leather chair to the left of the podium. He, too, was being moved by the music, until he looked up and saw Simon standing in the rear of the church. The pastor suddenly looked uncomfortable. He remembered Simon from when he and Dr. April Waters spoke with him at police headquarters. He did not expect to see him at church. Pastor Vincent did not know that he was the only person who could see him.

As the choir continued to sing, the pastor wondered why Simon was standing in the rear of the church and just staring at him. The way that Simon was looking at him, Pastor Vincent surmised that either Simon was expecting to see something, or he was about to cause something to happen. Pastor Vincent had seen him on television perform the Japan Miracles, and he hoped that Simon had not come to the church to start trouble. After what he witnessed on television, Pastor Vincent realized that there seemed to be very little that Simon could not do and that is what worried him.

"I have not come to start trouble, but I am expecting something from you," said Simon telepathically.

The pastor was startled and almost jumped from his chair. He looked around, wondering where the voice came from. It was definitely Simon's voice, and it sounded as if he were right next to him. When he looked up, Simon was still standing in the rear of the church.

"I can hear your thoughts," said Simon, *"and you can hear mine."*

"What do you want from me?" asked the pastor softly.

"You look a little silly talking to yourself. We can hear each other's thoughts. You don't need to move your lips, especially since you are the only one who can see me."

"Why are you here? What do you want?"

"I want you to repent," said Simon. *"Confess your sins of infidelity, declare your unworthiness, and step down from the ministry."*

"You can't be serious."

"Confess your sins of infidelity, declare your unworthiness, and step down from the ministry," repeated Simon.

"Right here and right now?" asked the pastor.

"Yes, right here and right now."

"I will repent. I promise I will. This is not the time or the place though."

"You know what the bible says about fake prophets, false teachers, and those who cause others to stumble. It would be better if you had a millstone tied around your neck and you were thrown into the sea. Your fate will be worse than that if you don't repent this very night."

"I admit to my sins," said the pastor, *"but I am not teaching false doctrine. I love the Lord, and I preach the Gospel as it is written. I don't change the words that are written or use it for personal gain."*

"That is not true," said Simon. *"The woman who is not your wife became attracted to you when she heard you preach. She mistook your arrogance for passion.*

You used the words of the Lord to sin. You have even quoted Scripture to her in bed while your wife thought you were visiting the sick. Jesus said how can you say you love me when you don't do as I ask?"

Pastor Vincent looked as if he had taken a blow to the stomach. He was dumbfounded and was having a hard time catching his breath. His eyes started to tear up, and he took a handkerchief from his jacket pocket and wiped them. The congregation assumed that he had been moved by the singing. Simon had forced him to look in the mirror, and once again, he wasn't prepared. He did not like what he saw.

"The choir will finish soon," said Simon. *"You have to make a decision. This is a life-or-death decision. Don't let your pride cause you to make the wrong choice."*

The pastor was agonizing over his situation, but he knew what he had to do. Deep down he knew that Simon was right, but he would have liked to have been able to end things on his own terms. To make matters worse, the church was almost filled to capacity, and his family was present. Some of his friends and coworkers were also in attendance. As the choir finished their last song, the pastor gathered himself, leaned over to the senior pastor, Reverend Tucker, and told him to be ready to speak in his place. He told him that he was unworthy. The senior pastor looked confused. When the singing ended, Pastor Vincent walked up to the podium with his Bible in his hand.

"God is good all the time, and all the time God is good," began Pastor Vincent. "It is certainly a pleasure and a privilege to be standing before you this evening. Your choir has certainly set the mood for worship. Please give your choir a big round of applause."

The congregation followed the pastor's instruction and gave the choir a big round of applause.

"Before I go any further, I want to ask the church for prayer. I am going through some things personally, and I need the people of God to pray for me. I had a word for you this evening, but God has instructed me to make a confession, and that is what I am going to do.

First, I want to let you know that I will be leaving the ministry. I am not sure at this moment if it will be temporary or permanent. I will pray on that."

He looked toward the back of the room at Simon. He hoped that Simon would give him some indication about his future in the church. Simon did not offer any help. He stood perfectly still and continued to look at the pastor as if to be saying stop stalling. Meanwhile, the congregation was taken by surprise. Pastor Vincent's family was also shocked and had to ward off questions from parishioners who sat next to them. The congregation began to quietly speculate about what was going on.

"You see, my brothers and sisters, I have sinned against God. Sometimes pastors are placed on a pedestal, and sometimes it goes to our head, and we are unable to handle it. We are held to a higher standard as we should be because we are called by God. This is hard for me to say in church, but I have not been faithful to my wife, which means I have not been honest with you. From the pulpit, I have instructed you to follow the word of God, but I have been following the ways of the world."

The low murmur became a loud gasp. Pastor Vincent's wife dropped her head and began to cry. A few people around his wife attempted to console her. The majority of the congregation was in shock and sat silently. They wanted to hear what else Pastor Vincent had to say. A few people in the congregation stood up and instructed the pastor to leave now. Pastor Vincent paused for a few moments as the ushers were able to get the congregation to calm down.

"I want to apologize to my wife, to my family, and all of you. I have no excuses. My wife is a wonderful woman, and my behavior has nothing to do with her. I am human, and the flesh is weak. I am also a man of God, and I know how Satan works. I should have had more discipline, and I should not have listened to his voice. Needless to say, I will not be bringing you the message tonight. Your senior pastor, Reverend Tucker, will do so instead. As I said earlier, please pray for me and my family. Once again, I am sorry and God bless."

Pastor Vincent took a quick glance at Simon before grabbing his Bible and leaving the pulpit. He walked to a nearby door and exited the church. Reverend Tucker grabbed his Bible and made his way to the podium. He appeared a bit flustered and unprepared. Pastor Vincent had put him in a pretty tough spot. Although he had had to speak many times on short notice, he has never had to follow such a shocking and unexpected announcement. Not knowing what else to do, Reverend Tucker started with a prayer. While praying, he decided what his topic should be. His message would be about forgiveness. Just like Jesus had done, he will challenge those who have never sinned to throw the first stone.

Once outside, Pastor Vincent thought about waiting for his wife near her car because he knew that she would be out soon. He was sure that after his announcement, she would not stay for the rest of the service. They had driven separately because she had a prior commitment. Ultimately, he decided to go on home and wait for his wife there. He was not exactly sure how she would react, but if it went badly, he did not want it to happen in the middle of the church parking lot.

Pastor Vincent headed to his car and was surprised to see Simon standing in front of it. He thought that Simon would want to speak to him once more before he left, but he had hoped to be gone before Simon showed up again.

"Did I miss something?" asked Pastor Vincent sarcastically.

"No, you did quite well. However, you are incorrect about one thing."

"What is that?" asked the pastor.

"Your wife is staying for the entire service. Reverend Tucker is talking about forgiveness, and she felt obligated to at least listen, even though she is hurting and embarrassed. I have a more important question for you: Are you ending the other relationship?"

"Yes, of course, I am. It has been bugging me for a while, and I

198

have been trying to figure out the best way to end it. If it was my choice, I would not have ended it like I did tonight, in front of the whole world. However, you are right. It should never have happened in the first place. Tell me if my wife will forgive me."

"That will depend on you. However, I will say this. It is a good sign that she decided to stay and listen to the message on forgiveness. That should be some consolation to you."

"That's a good sign. I hope I haven't lost her. What should I do?"

"Pray and be obedient to the Lord's direction."

"Why won't you help me?"

"I have given you the best possible advice. I hope you will follow it. As for me, there is a doctor friend of yours I need to speak with."

"What doctor friend? I don't have any doctor friends."

Pastor Vincent thought for a moment and remembered where he first met Simon. It was at police headquarters when he was called and asked to see if he could reason with him.

"Are you referring to Dr. April Waters?" asked the pastor.

"Yes, I am," said Simon. "You, however, should go home and wait for your wife and be sure to listen to her when she speaks. Listen not just with your ears but with your heart, also."

Pastor Vincent thought hard about what Simon had just said. Maybe he was giving him the help he asked for. He knew that he had to pray, but the pastor considered this last piece of advice priceless. He had some explaining to do, but now it was time to listen to his wife and acknowledge her feelings. Pastor Vincent watched Simon walk away and was amazed at his wisdom, his intelligence, and his relationship with Christ. He began to admire Simon.

Simon heard the pastor's thoughts as he walked away. Be careful what you wish for thought Simon. He considered it truly an honor to serve Christ, and he was very appreciative and grateful for the opportunity. He was also very lonely. I would love to have a family to go home to, he thought. Simon stopped and looked up at the sky.

"Forgive me, Lord. The evil one is trying hard to separate us. That will never happen. Get thee behind me, Satan."

Simon walked off into the night with a heavy heart. He was glad that Pastor Vincent made the right decision, but he could not get family out of his mind. It had been a while since Simon felt this way, and each attack of loneliness became stronger and harder to fight off. He knew he needed to have a heart-to-heart talk with Jesus about this but now was not the time. He needed to finish his assignment before the night was over, and he had to stay focused for that. Simon prayed a silent, quick prayer, asking for strength and discipline. He felt better almost immediately.

Time passed quickly for Simon as he was preoccupied with his thoughts. He was now standing right in front of police headquarters and had been there for a few minutes. Dr. April Waters had been analyzing an inmate the last couple of days. She was working late tonight to finish all the paperwork for the case. Simon paused before entering the building. He had to forget about his own concerns for now and focus on the assignment at hand. He wondered if his strong bouts of loneliness were because Satan was tormenting him or because Jesus was reminding him that he was still human.

Simon entered the building and walked through the lobby unnoticed—not because he blended in or because everyone was too busy to notice him, but because he willed it. Just like his visit with the pastor, Dr. Waters would be the only person who would be able to see him. As he walked through the lobby, he stopped and looked at a large bulletin board covered with glass. He saw many pictures tacked to the board under the word "Wanted." Simon stared at the pictures for a few moments and knew that some of them would be assigned to him. Dr. Waters' office was on the fourth floor, and Simon went straight to it.

Dr. Waters' desk faced her office door. She was busy on her computer, making notes about her current case. Every so often she would print a document and place it into a file folder. Simon stood in the doorway and watched her work. He noticed that she would occasionally lose her concentration and stop for a moment or two, drop her head, take a deep breath, and then continue. He listened to her thoughts, and just as at their first meeting, he knew that she was experiencing some internal conflict. He knew that she had been dealing with it for a long time.

"Shouldn't you be at home relaxing?" asked Simon.

Dr. Waters almost jumped out of her seat. She was so preoccupied with her thoughts, and her work that she had no idea anyone else was in the room. She let out a low-pitch squeal and knocked folders and papers from her desk. Her heart was pounding so hard that she placed both of her hands on her chest and looked at Simon in disbelief. His red hands were a giveaway, and she recognized him immediately. She was a nervous wreck, and it took her a minute to find her voice.

"I did not mean to frighten you. I am not here to harm you. You look tired. You should be at home with your daughter."

"What are you doing here? How did you get in? Don't you know that you are a wanted man? If I scream loud enough, every officer in the building will come running to my office?"

"I am only wanted by a few law enforcement officers who will soon become my allies. Attempting to scream will be futile. No sound will come out of your mouth. Your office phone is of no use to you either, and your cell phone has lost its charge. I am here to help you not harm you."

The more Simon talked, the more frightened she became. She tried to scream, but just as Simon said, no sound came from her mouth. She picked up her desk phone only to discover that there was no dial tone. She checked her cell phone, but it was dead. She could not help but look at Simon's red hands, and she imagined the worse.

"What do you want with me? I don't need any help from you or anyone else."

"You work a lot of hours because you are afraid to sleep. When you try to sleep, you have bad dreams. You blame yourself for your daughter being autistic, and you feel guilty because you're able to help others, but you can't help your own daughter."

"Mr. Simon, or whomever you claim to be, you are all over the television for what occurred in Japan recently. You appear to have some sort of magical power, which I think is all smoke and mirrors. Now, you're trying to analyze the psychologist. Exactly what do you want with me? What interest would someone like you have with me?"

"Only a few who saw what happened in Japan saw me. God will get the glory. I told you that I am here to help you."

"I told you that I don't need help with anything. Even if I did, why would you want to help me and why should I believe you?"

"That's the problem in a nutshell. There are a lot of things that you don't believe in, including Jesus. The sad thing is that you once were on fire for Jesus. To answer your question more specifically, I was sent here by someone whom you don't believe in to help you with something you say you don't need help with. I am here to rekindle that fire you once had."

"I think you're the one who needs help. I tell you what. I might listen to you if you can tell me something personal in which there is no way that you should know. I'm not talking about that story you were telling us at the police station when we first met. Everything you said about me had been in print. I don't know how you knew about Pastor Vincent's affair, but that could have been grapevine gossip. What do you think you know about me?"

"I know about the dreams that keep you awake at night and that you have never shared them with anyone."

"What are you referring to?" asked Dr. Waters, followed by a pause and an intense eye-to-eye challenge.

"I am talking about the recurring dream you have of your mother's death."

"My mother's accidental death was also in the newspaper."

"Yes, it was, but what was not in print is the argument you had with your mother right before she fell down the steps and broke her neck. Should I go on?"

202

"What more is there to say?"

"There is plenty more," said Simon. "Your mother disagreed with your plans to move in with your boyfriend. She tried to talk you out of it. She tried to scare you out of it by telling you that you would get pregnant and that your child would not be right if you lived in sin."

"That's enough!" ordered Dr. Waters as she covered her face with both hands and began to cry.

"Your mother became very upset when you told her that you were pregnant and that you and your boyfriend, David, planned to get married. You and your mother got into a heated argument, and your mother decided to go downstairs to cool off. As she walked toward the stairs, she was looking back at you, still scolding you. She was closer to the stairs than she realized, missed the step, and suffered a terrible fall, which broke her neck and killed her instantly."

The more Simon talked the harder Dr. Waters cried. Those memories came flooding back to her. She pulled a couple of tissue from a box on her desk and blew her nose. She threw the tissue in a nearby trash can, pulled out a couple more, and dabbed at her eyes.

Simon continued, "To make things worse, David was stabbed and robbed a couple of months after your mother died. His wounds were fatal, and he died in the very hospital where his child would be born. And if that wasn't enough grief, you almost had a nervous breakdown when the doctors told you that your daughter was autistic. You noticed that something wasn't quite right with her when she was two years old, so you took her to the doctor to have her examined. After a few days of testing, the doctors diagnosed her with autism. You went to counseling to deal with the grief and anger that you had experienced. You were upset because you thought that your mother had cursed you, but you are a very good mother. You should never doubt that. You think that the counselor who treated you sparked your desire to become a psychologist, but that is not true."

"What do you mean that is not true? That is absolutely true. I wanted to help people the way that psychologist helped me."

"That counselor didn't spark your desire to become a psychologist. Your mother is the reason you wanted to become a psychologist. She influenced you more than anyone. Your mother always wanted to become a psychologist but was not able to after she became pregnant with you. Don't you remember the talks the two of you had when you were a child? She asked you about your dreams and shared her dreams with you. You had always wanted to help people, but you talked about being a nurse when you were a child. Your mother wanted to study psychology."

"Oh my God!" exclaimed Dr. Waters. "You're right! That was so long ago, and so much has happened in my life that I almost forgot about those conversations."

"Your subconscious did not forget. After a couple of years of hearing your mother's stories, you changed your mind and wanted to become a psychologist. You wanted to make your mother proud of you. The counselor who treated you simply reignited those desires."

"Why didn't I remember that?"

"You were too busy feeling sorry for yourself and forgetting the good things about your mother. You focused on the negative. Your mother was just being a mother. She wanted you to have a better life than she had, which is what all parents want for their children. She wanted you to get your education before you started a family. Your mother tried to use psychology to scare you out of moving in with your boyfriend. What I want you to know is that the autism that your daughter has had nothing to do with your actions or what your mother said. Your daughter will live a long and prosperous life."

"Really!" exclaimed Dr. Waters. "What are you saying? How can you possibly know that?"

"The same way I know everything else about you. Jesus has allowed me to tell you that for your own mental health."

"My mental health is fine. Why do you think telling me this will draw me closer to Jesus? Why would I believe in a God who is described as love, but allows children to suffer? That is not the description of a loving God."

"That's the way your daughter's life began. That's not the way it will end. Your daughter will make you proud."

"What are you talking about?"

"Your daughter will go on to do great things. I don't know specifically what she will achieve. We both know that your daughter is excelling academically. In fact, her doctors have already told you that your high school sophomore can easily excel as a college sophomore, but you are still contemplating if you want her to make that jump."

"I don't know how you know all of these things," said Dr. Waters, "but there doesn't seem to be much that you don't know. I am still debating that move because I don't want Autumn to be looked at as some kind of circus freak. She already has a hard time fitting in socially, and I'm afraid those problems will magnify if she moves up four years in school."

"That will not happen to Autumn," said Simon.

"How do you know it won't?"

"You have to trust me. You just said that there seems to be very little that I don't know. This is one thing I do know. Besides, you are still focusing on the negative. You are not looking at the positive."

"I don't see a positive side to this."

"That has to change," said Simon. "As a very observant psychologist, you have noticed that Autumn appears to come out of her shell when she is challenged academically. She is happier and more comfortable than she has ever been. She is not only happy but also excelling the way you did when you became the youngest licensed psychologist in the country. You also have to stop blaming yourself for your child's autistic condition."

Again, Dr. Waters seemed to be somewhat stunned. Simon was correct about her daughter's academic achievements. The fact that she was not responsible for her daughter's autism had gone right over her head. She still wasn't sure if she could believe Simon about that, or about Autumn doing great things. For the first time in a long while,

April Waters was speechless. Simon had taken all the argument out of her. However, there was one thing that still bothered her.

"Even if I believe everything you have just told me, there is still one unresolved matter that I don't believe even you can fix."

"You're referring to your mother's death. You're still feeling guilty and blaming yourself for her accident."

"Yes, I am, because it is true. If she had not been so angry at me, she would have been watching where she was walking and would not have fallen down the stairs."

"You were very close to your father before he passed, weren't you?"

"Yes, I was, but what does my father have to do with my mother's death?"

"Do you remember the nickname your father had for your mother?"

"Yes, it was…" Dr. Waters stopped in midsentence. She looked at Simon in awe as tears flowed down her face. She covered her face with both hands again and sobbed uncontrollably. Simon allowed her to get more than sixteen years of pain out of her system. Dr. Waters now realized why he had asked about her father, and the answer freed her from years of pain. She regained her composure and proceeded to answer Simon's question, just to hear it come out of her own mouth.

"My father used to call my mother lefty because she was always stumbling and occasionally falling. He said that she was clumsy and walked as if she had two left feet. He swore that her clumsiness would be the death of her one day, and apparently, he was right."

"That's exactly correct. Your mother's death was not your fault. Jesus still wants to rekindle that fire in you. You should talk to him."

Simon turned and started walking out of the room. As he did so, the papers and file folders that Dr. Waters had knocked to the floor began to float back to the top of her desk and returned to the exact order in which they were before they hit the floor. Dr. Waters was again speechless and could only watch Simon as he left.

CHAPTER 20

GOD IS GOOD

Simon left the police station the same way he entered it—unnoticed. He saw Lieutenant Perkins pass through the lobby as he left, but he did not make himself noticeable to him. The lieutenant was in a hurry to book a suspect who had been wanted for months. Every officer in the station stopped what he or she was doing and watched the Lieutenant pass by with the handcuffed criminal. Lieutenant Perkins had never brought anyone in by himself. He always had backup. He nodded his head and spoke to every officer he made eye contact with. Simon smiled as he left the building. The lieutenant had listened to him.

The night was clear, and the sky was full of stars. Simon loved nights like this because it made him think of heaven. On these clear, starry nights, he liked to go to high ground, where nothing obstructed his view, and just gaze up into the sky. He decided to do just that. He walked to the tallest building downtown and transported himself to the roof.

He loved being high above the city. It was so quiet and peaceful and beautiful. The different colored lights of the city, and on the bridge were breathtaking, but the light created by the stars took him back to his homeland. For as long as he could remember, he loved looking up at the stars on a clear night. Even before he knew Jesus, he knew that the stars were special. To Simon, the stars symbolized something greater than man. Now he knew what that something was.

Each star looked as if it were trying to outshine the next one. The way they twinkled and blinked sometimes made Simon think they were winking at him. The different constellations they formed were nothing less than God's fingerprints. Every once in a while, Simon would see a shooting star. Humans had a scientific explanation for a shooting star, but Simon always wondered where God was sending it and why. What was its purpose other than its own beauty?

"You do beautiful work, Lord," said Simon.

"Thank you, My friend," replied Jesus. *"It's good to take time to enjoy creation every once in a while, but we still have more work to do."*

"Yes, Lord we do, but I am so amazed at what you have allowed me to accomplish with the people in this town. They are so hurt and fragile and confused, but through your wisdom and your grace, they have changed."

"Confused is a good term for their predicament. However, I hope you noticed that their confusion was not always their fault. It was often how they were raised. The parents will have to answer for their sins."

"Speaking of parents," said Simon, "thank you for sparing John Crenshaw's grandson. He was so devastated when he lost his son, and I wasn't sure that he would ever be emotionally stable again. I was really curious how you would respond when he asked to see how his son's death would benefit others."

"Did you doubt Me?"

"Not at all, but I did wonder how You were going to pull it off. You never cease to amaze me. The Japan Miracles were awesome. I felt so powerful and invincible when You worked through me to accomplish those miracles. I see how a little bit of power can go to someone's head. If man had experienced the power that you allowed me to experience, the earth would have been destroyed a long time ago."

"That sounds pretty bad, but you are correct about that," said Jesus.

"You did not reveal to me that some of the people who were

resurrected in Japan would not have a kidney. The man who does not have a heart was pure genius. You are truly an awesome God."

"You handled that situation very well. Your answer was perfect. I did not put those words in your mouth. You are a fast learner."

"I am whatever you tell me to be, my Lord. I am grateful that you chose to work through me to help others. It is so gratifying to see someone turn their life around and dedicate it to You. Everyone in this town whom you have allowed me to help is an unwavering testimony to Your grace and mercy."

"There is one thing they all have in common. Do you know what it is?"

"What is that, my Lord?"

"They had all been introduced to Me at an early age, and a major life event caused them to push away from Me. However, their parents planted the seed in them early, so they were still somewhat open to receiving Me again. This will not be true with some of your next assignments."

"Are you saying they will be more difficult to convert?"

"I am saying that you won't be able to convert some of them, but even knowing that you must continue to offer Me to them. I want you to be prepared because it will be harder for you. I know that you went through some difficult moments."

"Lord, you know everything about me. You know that I am a family man, and even though it's been centuries since I have been in a family situation, I still miss them."

"You asked me not to wipe your family from your memory. Do you remember making that request?"

"Yes, Lord, I remember."

"Have you changed your mind?"

"No, Lord, I have not. As I go about my service for You, I long to have a family to come home to at night. I realize this is a sacrifice I chose because nothing in my life comes before You, not even my family. It's just so hard."

"I have some news that may cheer you up," said Jesus.

"I can use a little cheering up about now."

"You remember the Crenshaw family whom you spoke of a little while ago?"

"Yes, Lord, I do. They are a great family. What about them?"

"John Crenshaw is a direct descendant of your family."

Simon could not believe his ears. He liked the Crenshaw family, and to learn that they are related to him truly was good news. Simon stared at the stars as if he were making direct eye contact with Jesus. He was thrilled that he was allowed to help his own family.

"I am speechless, Lord," said Simon.

"I have not revealed to you the best part about this news," said Jesus.

"I don't see how it can get any better, and I thank You, Lord, from the bottom of my heart. What can You possibly tell me that can be better than knowing I have family close by, even if they don't know we're related?"

"They don't know they are related to you, but they are very grateful to you. Rose, the daughter of John and the mother of Trey will have twin boys soon. She will name those boys Rufus and Alexander."

"Those are the names of my sons!" exclaimed Simon.

"Of course, they are," said Jesus. *"Rose, out of gratitude and appreciation wanted to do something to repay you for saving their family, but she did not know what she could do. Her parents told her about you. Though they gave Me the credit, she still wanted to honor you for your part in bringing her father back to Me. When she found out that she would be having twins, she began researching your life. When she found out that you had two sons, she knew right then how she would repay you. She would name her twins after your two sons."*

"This is beyond my wildest dreams," said Simon as a tear rolled down his left cheek. "Thank you, Lord. Thank you! I know that I will not be able to spend time with them or play with them, but I will be able to look in on them from time to time. I can't put into words how grateful I am to know that my family survived the atrocities that my country went through. I don't need to know how my family survived the journey to this land. I am just glad that they survived whatever challenges they had to face."

"I am glad that you are feeling better, My friend."

"I am feeling wonderful," said Simon. "I can't remember the last time I shed a tear. But these are tears of joy. People should know that their hope lies in You. Why can't the world see You and experience You and love You for who You are?"

"The world does not want to acknowledge the truth," said Jesus, "and I am the truth. The day will come when all people will be judged by the truth, and on that day, the world will be forced to acknowledge me."

William I. Brazley, Jr.